PAUL TREMBLING

LOCAL POET

HE KILLED HER. BUT WHO WAS SHE?

LION FICTION

Published by Lion Fiction
an imprint of
Lion Hudson plc
Wilkinson House, Jordan Hill Road
Oxford OX2 8DR, England
www.lionhudson.com/fiction

ISBN 978 1 78264 230 5
e-ISBN 978 1 78264 231 2

First edition 2016

Acknowledgments
Cover photo: Sally Mundy / Trevillion Images

A catalogue record for this book is available from the British Library

Printed and bound in the UK, September 2016, LH26

CONTENTS

CONTENTS

DAY 1: RTC

I was never much of a reader before Laney Grey touched my life. Not even newspapers. I got what I needed in the way of information or entertainment from TV, or off the net. On holiday I might pick up a thriller to read on the beach, but if I didn't finish it in that week or so, I probably never would.

And I certainly didn't read poetry. Not since school, anyway. My English teacher had made earnest attempts to open my young mind to our rich literary heritage, but he was doomed to failure. On the back row of the classroom, poetry appreciation never progressed beyond dubious limericks.

There's no reason to believe that anything would ever have been different if Laney hadn't catalysed change. It wasn't as if I was discontented with my life. There were no inner yearnings for depth and meaning, no navel-gazing angst about some undefined need. The truth is that I was perfectly happy with things as they were.

Then Laney stepped so briefly into my life, and so swiftly out of hers.

I only really saw her for one fractional moment. A young woman, smooth dark skin and frizzed hair, stepping out from behind a parked car into the spray and driving rain from a sudden shower, and then another step out into the road before just stopping. She was looking at me, water running down her cheeks, but no surprise or shock in her face. There were just those dark eyes, meeting mine, and in my memory they were huge and deep and calm, though no picture ever showed that. No photo ever captured what I saw in that moment; what I still see when I think of her.

I don't remember the actual impact, or anything that happened immediately after. I was told that my van was doing about forty when it hit her, and the impact flung her ten feet in the air. When she came down, her head struck first, on the asphalt. She had a cracked skull and a broken neck and a ruptured spleen, and both lungs were pierced by broken ribs. She was already dead when I reached her and picked her up and held her. They say I was pleading with her, begging her to live, and trying to give her mouth-to-mouth. They say that my tears were mixing with the rain and her blood, soaking together into my T-shirt and her denims.

But I can't remember any of that.

The rest of that day comes back to me only in a jumble of disconnected images. I can remember being at hospital. I can remember asking, "How is she?... Will she make it?" I think I must have been asking that a lot, but I don't remember what answers I got. I suppose I was there to be checked myself, because later on I had a dressing over my right eye. I don't remember it being put on, or how I got the injury.

I know I spoke to the police. Of course, they had to investigate. They had me blow into something, but I hadn't had a drink since the previous evening, so it must have been negative. At some point they told me that they were taking the van away for forensic tests. And they asked a lot of questions. I don't remember what.

The one clear thing in all that time was how I felt. The desperate fear that I had done something terrible; that I had taken a life. The fear that slowly shaded into despair as I realized that she was dead. I suppose someone must have told me. Perhaps I was told several times.

Eventually they said I was OK. The coppers took me down to the nick, and I realized that I'd been arrested. They booked me in, gave me a cup of tea, and sat me in a cell. I was feeling too numb to care.

I'm not sure how long I was there for. Somewhere along the line they brought in a meal – nothing fancy, just something microwaved. Since that and takeaways are mostly what I eat anyway, I had no complaints, and I felt better for having eaten. My brain began to work again, and I could start to remember events more coherently.

Shortly after that they took me for a formal interview. Two coppers: a young lad who said very little and a stocky blonde woman who introduced herself to me and the tape as PC June Henshaw.

"Can you confirm your name, please?" she asked formally.

"Seaton. Robert David Seaton. And it was an accident. Really. She just stepped out in front of me."

Henshaw raised an eyebrow. "You didn't seem so sure when we talked to you at the hospital."

"I know. I was confused. Couldn't think straight. Shock, I suppose." I shrugged. "Now I've had time to think, it's clearer. Some of it. I don't remember the… the actual…"

Somewhat to my surprise I found myself choking up at that point. Her face was suddenly clear in my mind, staring calmly at me as I bore down on her, my foot jamming the brake down as hard as I could while I heaved on the wheel.

"I tried to brake. I tried to turn. She was just too close."

PC Henshaw nodded. "Do you remember how fast you were going?"

"Forty. No more than that. The speed cameras along that stretch are lethal. Those average speed things. A lot of my mates have been caught out by them, so I'm always careful along there."

"You use that road a lot?"

I nodded. "Part of my regular route."

"I see. Well, Mr Seaton, what you've told me is consistent with what we've heard from several witnesses, and other evidence."

That sounded hopeful. "Other evidence?" I asked, anxious to hear that my story had been confirmed.

"We've reviewed CCTV footage – we were lucky, there's a camera near the scene that was pointing that way. And RTC

Investigation have given us an initial report. It all confirms that she stepped out in front of you and that you had no chance of avoiding the collision."

It seems ridiculous to say that a weight lifted off me, but that's exactly what it felt like.

"We may have to ask you more questions later. There will be an inquest at some point, and I expect you will be required to give evidence then. But for now, you're free to go."

"So – I'm not under arrest any more?"

She shook her head and she smiled. Just a faint smile, but it lightened her face, turned her into a different person. "No. We're dropping the charges. Pending further inquiries, that is. Your van will have to be examined, to rule out any mechanical problems that may have contributed to the accident. And there are still some witnesses I need to speak to. But we have no reason to detain you any further."

"Thanks." That sounded a bit too casual somehow, so I said it again. "I mean – really, thanks." I shook my head, not sure what I wanted to say.

"That's OK; just doing our job. It's been a pretty bad day for you, hasn't it, Mr Seaton?" She smiled again, with the same effect as before, but this time she was conveying sympathy. "Understatement of the year! But if you need to talk to someone about this, I can put you in touch with an independent counsellor."

I shook my head. Where I come from, blokes don't go to "counsellors". You man up and deal with it yourself. "No thanks."

"Do you have anyone you can talk to about it? Family or close friends?"

My closest living relative was a cousin in Blackpool. The last time we'd met he'd given me a black eye and I'd bloodied his nose; I was eight and he was nine or ten. I was currently "not in a relationship" and, although I had plenty of friends, I didn't want to talk to any of them just now.

"I'm fine," I told her.

She offered me a lift home, but I said I'd walk. It had stopped raining, I needed some space to clear my head, and my flat was only a mile from the police station.

I walked for more than an hour, going over it all in my mind. Thinking that if I'd seen her a moment sooner… if I'd been driving just a little slower… if I'd taken a different route. Planned my drops in a different order. Pulled a sickie and taken the day off. If, if, if.

But there was no if. There was only her face, her eyes meeting mine – the last thing she saw in this life.

When I came out of it, I was on a street I didn't recognize. I had to bring up Google maps on my phone to find out where I was, and it showed me further from home than when I'd started. I'd done enough walking. I called a taxi.

The driver gave me a strange look when he picked me up, and another as I was paying him after the short trip.

"You OK, mate?" he asked.

"I'm fine," I said for the second time that day.

It wasn't until I got inside and saw myself in the mirror that I understood his concern. My eyes were red and swollen, but tears were still trickling down my cheeks, and my blood stained T-shirt was sodden.

DAY 2: ACCUSATIONS

Next morning I woke up late. The first thing that came into my head was, "You killed someone yesterday." I wanted to go back to sleep and forget.

I couldn't, of course. Instead I just lay in bed with the thought going through my head: "You killed her, Rob. You. Robert David Seaton. You hit her with your van. You killed her."

After ten minutes of that, I was near to tears again. I didn't want to go there any more, so I got up, showered, and phoned work. They told me to take the day off. Several days if I needed them. It wasn't what I'd wanted to hear. I would have preferred to be with people and doing something. But there was no point in me going in anyway, as the police had taken my van. So I sat with a coffee and caught the last of the breakfast news.

It hadn't made headlines, of course. What's one more fatal RTC in a world full of major tragedy? The main stories were a natural disaster in the Far East and shoddy politics exposed in Whitehall. But the local news had a short piece on the death of Elaine Josephine Grey, a well-known poet.

I hadn't known her name. If I'd been told, it hadn't registered. I hadn't known that she was a poet. I wouldn't have known it was her at all except for the picture they showed.

I dressed and went out to the paper shop for milk and the local rag. It had a bit more information, mostly details of the accident, but some background about her as well. I read it through several times over my cereal.

Elaine Josephine Grey, better known as Laney. Thirty years old, two years younger than me. Born and bred in this part of town, went to school just down the road from my flat. She'd been writing then, writing some quality stuff, it seemed. At fourteen she'd won a national competition. But the early promise had faded. The article recorded nothing else until she published her first book of poems, twelve years later. There had been two more since.

The reporter made much of her contribution to the cultural life of the community, making particular mention of her readings for charity and the poetry workshops she'd run in schools and community centres. Her death was such a tragedy, such a pointless waste.

It hurt to read that. Not that there was any suggestion of blame. My name wasn't even mentioned, which I was glad about. The article merely said that the police investigation was continuing. Nevertheless, the thought that I had caused this loss left me somehow hollow inside. As though part of me had died with Laney.

I dug out my laptop and went online. The first thing my search brought up was her website. Why was I surprised to find she had her own site? Just about everybody did nowadays. Everybody except me, perhaps. In any case, there it was: "Laney's Lounge". The usual sort of stuff. Photos, a short bio that added nothing to the newspaper report and was probably its main source. Some samples of her work that I skipped over, links to her books on Amazon, an itinerary. I looked too closely at that. She was supposed to be leading a poetry workshop today.

She had a blog as well. Last entry four weeks ago. Something about the frustration involved in being a poet. It wasn't something I connected with, so I skimmed over it, and moved on to the forum.

There were a lot of threads listed, covering a range of topics to do with poetry in general and Laney's poems in particular. But the most recent thread was labelled "In Memory". It had been up for less than twenty-four hours, but it was already the longest one, as people who had known Laney poured out their shock and sorrow and incomprehension at the suddenness of the tragedy.

I scrolled down, not wanting to read them but feeling that I was somehow obligated to give them some attention. I had to acknowledge what I had done. But neither could I go through them in detail. Instead, I glanced through them, picking up words and phrases here and there. Many of them repeated.

"Heartbroken…"

"Shocked…"

"Tragic…"

"Murder…"

That pulled me up short with a sudden twist in my guts. I read the entire post. Just one sentence: "I just hope that the bastard who did it goes down for murder."

Underneath someone had added a correction: "Not murder. Manslaughter. And they'll get off with a slap on the wrist."

Further down I read: "Drunk driver, probably. Or on drugs. Hope he BURNS in HELL!"

I couldn't read any more. The screen had blurred, my cheeks were wet.

I wanted to apologize; to say I was sorry, it was an accident. I was sorry, sorry, sorry. I wanted to explain that I hadn't been drunk, hadn't been speeding. She just stepped out in front of me. I hadn't meant to hit her and I was so, so sorry. And I could have done that – added my message to the others. But instead I sat and stared numbly at the screen. I was afraid to expose myself to that level of anger, and I felt too guilty to defend myself effectively.

The ring on the doorbell was a welcome intervention, dragging me away from the accusing words on the screen. Discovering two coppers on my doorstep was a lot less welcome. Plain clothes; one a bit plainer than the other. The officer who introduced himself as DS Fayden was very sharply dressed: full three-piece suit, and it didn't look cheap either. The DC with him looked a little dowdy in comparison; DS was apparently higher up the pay scale than DC.

With the word "murder" still branded on my mind, I assumed that they were there to re-arrest me. But they reassured me on that point. Just a few more questions, they promised. A few points to clarify.

So I made tea, and went over it again. Where had I been going? How long had I been driving that day? Was I late? In a hurry? Was this a regular route? And so on. They were thorough, but didn't probe. Just asked the questions and moved on. All routine – at first.

But then the questions took a different direction, and a different tone. Had I known Ms Grey before? Had I ever met her? Did I know any of her family? Her friends? They asked all these several times, in different ways, talking in turns to rapid-fire their queries, keeping me off-balance. Fortunately, the answer was a simple "No" in each case. If I'd been lying I would have struggled to keep thinking of the answer.

They moved on to places I might have been where I could have met her. Names of people who might be connected to her. Did I know Kev Dixon? Sadie DeSallas? Ahmed Moshin, Cody Bryson, Dougie Keen? Anyone known as Jag, as Stubby, as Greek Johnnie…?

The last name finally rang a bell, though a faint one. Buffeted by the stream of questions, I couldn't have even thought about denying it, even if I'd wanted to.

"Johnnie Papadopoulos, you mean?"

"You know him, then?"

"Not well. Met him a few times, that's all. He used to drink at the Duke of Clarence, just down the road from here." I frowned, as memory kicked in. "Haven't seen him around for a while, actually. I did hear that he'd been sent down for supplying drugs. But what's that got to do with an RTC?"

The coppers exchanged a glance.

"There are aspects to the inquiry that we're not at liberty to discuss," said one of them. "But I think we've got all the information we need from you for the moment. We'll be in touch."

After they'd left, I slumped back down on the sofa, feeling emotionally drained. I couldn't understand the drugs thing at all – though it did at least explain why CID were involved.

I went back to the laptop, wondering if there was any connection between the online accusations and the CID visit. A new post had appeared, from someone calling themselves BookLady: "Dear, dear Laney. Your black gull finally landed, and we are all poorer because of it."

It made no sense to me. I went back to bed.

DAY 3 : THE WAVE

I had only meant to take a short nap. I woke up about three the following morning, fuzzy headed but unable to go back to sleep. The remnants of a dream were still hanging around my consciousness as a vague sense of unease and the image of a black seagull.

I made some strong coffee and sat puzzling over it. As is normal with dreams, the harder I tried to remember it, the more insubstantial the memory became, until I was no longer certain that the black gull had featured in the dream at all. Perhaps I had merely remembered it from the blog post? For something that made no sense, it was remarkably difficult to forget.

As the coffee took effect, it occurred to me that it might be a reference to one of Laney's poems. So I went back to the internet. I didn't want to face any more accusations, so I avoided her site. Instead, I did a search for her books.

All three were available, on several sites and in various formats. I also found some reviews of her work. They tended towards the positive, with a good number being downright enthusiastic, but none of them mentioned gulls of any colour.

Delivery of a paperback copy would take several days, and of course I didn't possess an e-reader. But they were also available as pdf files. On impulse, I downloaded one: *Postcards to Myself* – the first she had published.

I skipped over the opening pages, going straight to the first poem: "The Wave". That sounded like the sort of thing that might include seagulls.

Smoothly swelling muscle under shiny-wet skin…

It didn't seem much like a wave, I thought.

*Diamond-dust dancing along your head, each mote
a brief incandescence.*

I had to stop and look up "mote".

*You build yourself from the blue depths, gathering
strength…*

Finally, I realized that she was indeed talking about a wave. I felt inordinately pleased with myself for this small breakthrough. Nothing to this poetry thing, really.

Encouraged, I carried on reading. There was more about the wave. In fact it was all about the wave. Every second of its growth and development was described in minute detail, down to the streaks of foam and the varying shades of colour. It seemed a bit over the top to me. What was so special about this wave?

I skim-read down to the end, looking for the punchline. Slightly to my surprise, there was one. Or a sort of one. But it made no sense at all.

*"No personal items on your desk," says Mrs
Howard, wielding a bin with executive authority.
And the wave breaks, unseen, on a desolate shore.*

I had no idea where Mrs Howard had sprung from. But in any case, there was no mention of any gulls, black or otherwise. I gave up on the wave, and began skim-reading through the rest of the book.

Laney covered a lot of subjects. There was a poem about clouds, another about a bus journey. An amusing description of a party caught my attention – isolated snippets of conversation, overheard at random and linked together into something wildly improbable. And there was a lengthy piece about a chimney: a large Victorian one, left standing on its own in a demolition site.

Finally, I came across a gull. Not a black one; just ordinary grey and white. Laney described it with the same vivid detail she'd used to describe the wave. Sunlight on feathers, the cruel curve of its beak and the arrogance of its expression, its harsh and mournful cry.

But something was wrong with this bird. Its voice was not heard over empty sea, but in the cramped confines of a scruffy urban park. It didn't strut along a wide beach, but along the concrete rim of a rubbish-strewn pond. Its companions weren't other gulls and seabirds, but ducks and geese and pigeons and common sparrows.

And it didn't fly. It didn't soar. When it flapped, it did so with just one wing. The other was injured, torn and crippled. The gull was a prisoner in the park, a permanent refugee. Instead of riding the ocean winds, it must bicker with the other birds for scraps of bread and other rubbish. Its haughty gaze was all it had left of its previous life.

It was surprisingly effective. I found myself feeling a deep regret for the seagull's sad condition. But it didn't seem to have anything to do with the black gull, and it was the last poem in the collection.

Frustrated, I switched off. It was nearly seven. Time to be heading for work. Van or not, I needed to be doing something.

Work, for me, was just a five-minute walk away. When you spend all day driving, you don't need a long commute as well, so I'd found a flat nearby. The arrangement worked so well that I rarely drove my own car, which was quietly rusting away in a disused back corner of my workplace.

As usual for that time of day, some of the lads were still hanging around the office, having a cup of tea and winding up the office staff before they went out on their runs. I was gratified by their reaction when I turned up: rough-edged but genuine sympathy. The general attitude was "It could have been any one of us, mate". It was good to feel that I had people on my side – the label "murderer" still hung in my mind, as did the memory of the CID visit and their probing questions.

Colin, the operations manager, came bustling out of his office telling everyone they should have been out on the road five minutes ago – as he always did at that time. It was the main reason everyone hung round for an extra five minutes. The Morning Wind-Up was a genuine company tradition. He stopped short when he saw me.

"Ah. Rob. Wasn't expecting you today. Are you sure you're ready to be back at work?"

A fussy little man, Colin, always quoting various rules and regs to give himself a semblance of authority. He was saved from being a complete disaster as a manager by having a genuine loyalty to his staff, once you got past the jobsworth attitude.

"Need to be doing something, Col. I'm going nuts just sitting around all day."

He nodded. "Your van's not back yet, and I've split your run among all the others – SO THEY NEED TO GET GOING!" Once he started raising his voice, it was the signal that the game was over for the day, and the lads began cheerfully wandering out.

Authority reasserted, Colin nodded in satisfaction and turned back to me. "There is a little job you can do, if you're sure...?"

I was sure.

It was a one-off delivery to be made to a place not on any of our normal routes. We get a few jobs like that, and the firm keeps a Fiesta van for such purposes. It was all loaded up and ready to go. I just had to sign the keys out and make an easy ten-mile trip.

Except that when I got behind the wheel I started to shake.

"Get a grip!" I snarled. But when I closed my eyes I saw Laney, looking at me so calmly as she waited.

I opened them again. The Fiesta was visible from Colin's office. If I didn't get started soon he'd be down to see what the problem was.

I started the engine. Put it in gear. Reversed out into the yard. Concentrating hard on each action, refusing to think about anything other than exactly what I was doing. Living in the moment.

I drove carefully out of the gates, paused for a break in the traffic, and then turned into the street.

"I can do this!" I told myself. Then I noticed that I was gripping the wheel so tightly that my knuckles were white. "I can do this," I repeated, and forced myself to relax.

It should have taken me less than an hour there and back, including time to make the delivery, sort the paperwork, and have a cup of tea and a chat with the customer. It took me more than two. When I got out of the van my arms were aching from tension, and my shirt was stuck to my back.

Still, I felt as though I had won a victory of sorts. I could still do my job.

Not that there was much of a job for me to do just then. No more unscheduled deliveries needed. I hung around for a bit, trying to help out in the office but mostly getting in the way. So I went down to the warehouse and gave them a hand preparing orders for the next day. But they had the job pretty much covered, and before long I was at a loose end again. Enough was enough. I went and told Colin that I was calling it a day.

Still, it was a bit early to go home and sit in an empty flat. Instead, I walked for a while without going anywhere in particular, and struggling to resolve a problem.

Laney's death wasn't my fault. I knew that, and PC Henshaw had confirmed it. Stepping out into the road like that had been Laney's choice, not mine. But it had been my hands on the steering wheel, my foot on the accelerator, my van that had taken her life. Responsible or not, I couldn't get past that.

And in a way, I realized that I didn't want to. I didn't want to just shrug my shoulders and forget the whole thing. I couldn't just dismiss Laney like that. She had been a living person; someone who did things, felt things, just as I did. Somehow, that needed to be marked out.

But that left me feeling guilty for something that wasn't my fault. What was I supposed to do about that? I'd already ditched the idea of counselling. Wandering past a church, I thought about going in and having a word with the vicar. After all, the church was well clued up on guilt; that was part of its regular stock-in-trade.

I hesitated there for a moment. I hadn't been in a church since a mate had got married three years ago. I wasn't sure if I'd be comfortable opening myself up in such a place. Wouldn't that be just another form of counselling, with the added bonus of having God sitting in on the conversation?

An elderly lady coming out of the church gave me a suspicious look, which helped make my mind up. I moved on.

A little further down the road was a library. That gave me another idea. I couldn't change the past, I refused to ignore it, but I could at least explore it. If I could discover more about Laney, understand her and what she was saying in her poetry, that might be a way of at least acknowledging who she had been and what I had done.

Somehow, it felt right. So I went inside.

It wasn't until I was already past the doors before I remembered that I was even less familiar with libraries than I was with churches. I hadn't been in one since I was at school, and that had ended badly, when I was evicted for trying to stick someone to a chair with chewing gum. It had seemed funny at the time.

But it was too late to change my mind. The middle-aged lady behind the desk had already spotted me and was looking expectantly in my direction.

"How can I help you?" The fish symbol on her cardigan marked her out as a God-botherer; there was no getting away from them today. On the other hand, she had a warm smile and the question sounded genuine.

"I'm interested in poetry." To my ears, that sounded ridiculous. Did I look like the sort of person who read poetry? I half expected her to fall over laughing.

Instead her smile broadened, and she nodded enthusiastically. "Oh, good! I love poetry myself. Was there any particular sort you wanted to read?"

There were different sorts of poetry? "I wasn't really looking for something to read. I mean, I have been reading some. I was just looking for some help in understanding it."

This time she did laugh. "You want to understand poetry? You'd better have a lifetime or two to spare!" She leaned forward and lowered her voice. "I'll let you in on a secret, shall I? I've been reading poetry since I was a little girl, and a lot of it I still can't understand!"

"Then why..."

"Because it's not always about understanding. Sometimes it's just the flow of the words, the rhythm of them, the images they create. Sometimes I read poetry to enjoy the experience of reading poetry." She saw my mystified look and sighed. "And sometimes you can understand. It depends a bit on the poet. Was there anyone in particular you've been reading?"

I nodded. "Laney Grey."

Her eyes suddenly misted over. "Oh, yes," she said softly. "Laney. Dear, sweet Laney."

"You knew her!" It was meant as a question, but somehow came out almost as an accusation.

Fortunately, she took no offence. "Oh, yes. Very well. She often came here to do readings and workshops. She was here only last week."

A nod of her head indicated a small extension off the side of the room. It had been set out with a circle of chairs, one of them bearing a card with Laney's name and a black ribbon. There may have been other writing as well, but the rest of the card was obscured by the pile of flowers that covered the seat and overflowed onto the floor.

"It was only meant to be a little memorial by the staff here. Just our way of saying goodbye, I suppose. But so many people have added flowers and cards…"

I nodded, not trusting myself to speak.

"It's a tribute to how many lives she touched. And is still touching, I suppose. I'm afraid that all our copies of her books are out, but I can put your name on the waiting list if you like – Mr…?"

"Seaton. Rob Seaton."

"I'm…" She pointed towards her left breast. I looked, but saw only tightly stretched white linen. Seeing my confusion, she glanced down, and blushed. "I'm not wearing my name tag. Again! Sorry – Sandra Deeson."

We shared embarrassed smiles. "I wasn't looking to get a copy. I'm not even a member, actually. I downloaded one of her books onto my laptop, and I've read it – some of it – but I think I must be missing something."

Sandra nodded. "I know that feeling. The thing to remember with Laney's work – with a lot of poets, in fact – is that what you see isn't necessarily what you get."

I raised an eyebrow. "Sorry?"

"What the words say isn't what it's really about."

I turned the thought over in my mind, trying to find an angle from which it made sense. Sandra gave me a hopeful look, which I met with a slow head shake.

"OK, let's try an example. Which of her poems do you know best?"

"I suppose 'Wave' is the one I've read most."

She nodded enthusiastically. "Good choice! What did you think it was about?"

"Well, a wave, obviously. But there's that bit at the end with the waste bin – it doesn't fit!"

"So where's the waste bin?"

I thought back over the words. "It seems like it's in an office somewhere. But how do you get a wave into an office?"

"The same way that you get a lake into a library." She nodded at the wall behind her, where a calendar displayed a sunny view of Windermere.

"It's a picture?"

Sandra nodded, and there was almost an audible click in my mind as things fell into place.

"She's got a picture on her desk – a picture of a wave. A postcard, perhaps. And she's looking at the picture, thinking about the wave, when someone comes along and dumps the picture in a bin."

We exchanged smiles, equally thrilled by my breakthrough.

"So that's what it's about!"

Sandra replaced her smile with a frown. "Well, no. Not entirely. That's what happens, yes, but that's not what it's *about*."

My jaw may not have actually dropped, but it certainly sagged a little. "But…"

Before I could organize a sentence, a group of youngsters in school uniform made a dramatic entrance, chattering loudly. Sandra smoothly switched roles from tutor to sergeant major.

"This is a library! There will be no running and you will talk quietly or leave!"

The noise level dropped significantly, though children continued to pour through the door. Most dispersed down the aisles, but a large number began queuing behind me at the desk.

"Sorry about that. It's kicking out time at the school. We get a lot of the kids coming in while they wait for their bus or their parents. I'm going to be busy for a while… Here, if you fill this in and bring it back, I'll get your membership sorted out, then we can find some books to help you out."

I took the form and began to step aside, cultural conditioning making me conform to acceptable standards of queue behaviour. "So what is it about?" I asked as Sandra began taking books from her next customer.

She found time to give me a slightly harassed smile. "It's about being there," she said.

I walked home, which took about ten minutes and was enough time to give up on the whole poetry thing. PC Henshaw phoned me as I was walking through the door.

"Accident Investigation have finished with your van, and they haven't found anything that would have contributed to the incident. So you can make arrangements to collect the vehicle. Within twenty-four hours, ideally, or the garage starts adding storage charges."

"No problem. I'll pick it up tomorrow." The thought of driving again, especially in that van, set my guts churning. I suppressed my reaction. I would have to deal with it sooner or later. "Does this affect the investigation at all?"

"Not really. It just confirms what we already thought."

"Good. It's just that I've been reading some nasty comments lately, online. People saying it was a drunk driver and so on. They've even called me a murderer. It might help if you could put that straight. Officially."

"I'm sorry to hear that, but I'm afraid it's not unusual in cases like this. Feelings run high for a while. They should settle down quickly, though. But I'll arrange a press release; make it clear that we're not looking to bring any charges at present."

"Can't you just come straight out and say it was an accident?"

"Not until after the inquest, which might be a while yet, I'm afraid. It's up to the coroner to rule on whether or not it was accidental death. But I'll think about the wording – try to take some heat off you."

That was obviously the best I was going to get – unless the detectives had turned up something that would direct attention away from me. "What about the drugs angle?"

"Drugs?" Henshaw sounded surprised. "What drugs?"

"Well, it's just that the two plain-clothes officers who came to see me seemed very interested in a possible drugs connection."

There was a short but significant pause. "Mr Seaton – do I understand that CID officers have talked to you in relation to this incident?"

"Yes. The day after it happened. I thought you'd have known about it."

PC Henshaw's reply had the feel of someone choosing their words with extreme caution. "Yes. I would have expected to be informed. There may have been a breakdown in communications. Do you happen to recall the names of the officers?"

I had to think hard about it. They had told me, but I'd been more concerned at that point with the possibility of being arrested for murder. "There was a sergeant. DS Faden – something like that. And the one with him, unusual name, sounded Italian."

"Cadenti? DC Cadenti and DS Fayden, was it?"

"That's right."

There was a pause in our conversation, during which I could hear a few muffled noises. It sounded like someone swearing vigorously, having first covered the mouthpiece with their hand.

The noises stopped, and PC Henshaw returned to the phone. "I shall have to get back to you on this, Mr Seaton."

She hung up rather abruptly.

"A breakdown in communications, was it?" I said to myself, and reflected that it wasn't just poets who didn't mean what their words said.

The evening dragged a bit. I had a bite to eat, watched some TV. My own company became oppressive, so I went to the gym.

Sitting in a van all day will quickly turn you into a beached whale, especially on a fast-food diet, so I tried to do something healthy at least once a week. And there was something about a good sweaty workout that often lifted my mood. But not this time. Even after pounding the treadmill for half an hour, my thoughts still kept coming back to a broken body and blood soaking into the road.

I showered and went down to the pub, where I had a couple of pints, chatted to some people, watched some more TV. A football match was on, some European league game. After half an hour, I realized that I had no idea who was playing and didn't really care. I finished my drink and went home.

Having picked up a takeaway on the way back, I started eating while I searched the TV for something to watch. Halfway through my chicken korma I'd searched the entire Freeview channel list twice. I didn't want to watch TV. I didn't want chicken korma.

What I wanted was for the last few days to have never happened. I wanted Laney Grey to be alive and well, and someone I'd never heard of.

DAY 4: OFFICE WORK

Colin wasn't keen that I should go and collect my van, though I insisted that I was OK to do it.

"You can't take it out on a job yet anyway," he argued. "Our own mechanics have to check it over first."

"What for? There's nothing wrong with it. The police said so."

He shrugged. "Policy. I've no say in it. You're not even supposed to drive it till then."

"That's ridiculous!"

"If you want to argue with Head Office about it, feel free. In the meantime, I'll arrange for the van to be picked up, and I'll see if I can sort out a Fiesta run for you. Go and get a coffee or something."

When it came to matters of policy, Colin was immovable. I went and got a coffee.

I sat in the main office and sipped it. The staff there were friendly enough, but had no time for chit-chat. They were too busy hammering away on keyboards, sorting papers, making phone calls. Processing orders, I supposed. Strangely, though I must have been in there thousands of times in the years I'd worked for the firm, I only had a vague idea what they actually did.

Looking at the desks, it was clear that the terrible Mrs Howard had never been there. Mixed in with the papers and pens and other assorted officeware were a wide range of clearly personal items: family photographs, cartoons of office life, a solar-powered nodding dog.

I'd never noticed any of that before, either.

Presumably there was no company policy regarding what was allowed on desks, or Colin would have enforced it rigorously. However, lacking any guidance from higher authority, he seemed to have taken an "anything goes" attitude. In fact, now I thought about it, he had a couple of photos and a plastic flower on his own desk.

One of the office girls had a framed picture of a mountain hanging on the wall next to her. Not a photograph, an actual painting. I got up and took my coffee over for a closer look.

"Where's that, Liz?"

"Um?" She glanced up from the screen, followed my gaze, and looked at the painting. "Oh. Scotland. Had a holiday there a few years ago."

"Do you look at it?"

"Of course!" Her normally pleasant features were creased into a frown.

"Why?"

Her frown deepened. "Because it's nice to look at. And it's better than staring at Tim all day!"

Tim glanced up from his own desk, which faced Liz's. "I like to look at it too," he said. "It reminds me that there are better places. And nicer people."

She stuck her tongue out at him and turned back to me. "Rob, I'd love to sit and discuss art with you all day, but I'm a bit busy at the moment."

"Of course. Sorry."

I went and sat at a vacant desk and finished my coffee. There was a good atmosphere in the office, I thought. People were busy, but there was a lot of banter, a lot of smiles and laughs and chatter. I'd never worked in an office myself, but now I thought about it, some places must be pretty miserable to work in. Such as any office run by Mrs Howard.

I thought of Laney Grey working in an office. I thought of her looking at a picture of a wave. Not just glancing at it occasionally, as Liz did with her mountain, but staring into it, intent on seeing every detail. Building it in her mind – the sounds, the smells, the entire experience of the wave. Trying her best to be there...

... And then having it abruptly snatched away, dumped into a waste bin.

I felt it.

For one brief fraction of eternity, Laney reached out from behind the words and touched me with her boredom and loneliness and aching desire to escape; with her loss and desolation as her escape route was snatched away. For a moment, I knew exactly what it felt like to work in Mrs Howard's office.

"You OK, Rob?" Tim called from across the room, and I realized that I was sitting with my mouth gaping open.

"Yes. Fine thanks." I got up, took my mug out to the kitchen, and washed up, then went back to Colin's office and stuck my head round the door.

"Col – doesn't seem much point in me hanging round here. I'm just getting in the way. Call me if you need me back."

Colin glanced up. "Of course. Take any time you need, Rob."

"Thanks." I started to leave, then had a sudden impulse and turned back again. "Colin – if you don't mind me asking – why the plastic flower?"

"The flower?" He looked embarrassed. "My daughter gave it me years ago. She said it would brighten up my office. Never thought to get rid of it."

I nodded. "Don't. She was right. And by the way, Col – you run a good office."

"Oh. Er, thank you."

I left, leaving him looking pleased but slightly bemused.

I made a brief stop at my flat to find and complete the application form I'd been given, then made my way to the library, stopping at a florist's on the way.

To my disappointment, Sandra wasn't at the reception desk. A younger woman peered at me rather dubiously over the top of her glasses, accepted the form, and informed me that the machine that produced the library cards was broken and they'd have to send it away for processing. Should be ready in a day or two.

She became even more dubious when I asked after Sandra, and gave the bunch of flowers I was carrying a suspicious glance, but finally released the information that it was Sandra's day off and she'd be back tomorrow.

I was disappointed, since I was still bubbling with my revelation and desperately wanted to talk to someone about it. But today's librarian didn't seem likely to be interested, so I'd just have to keep it to myself.

However, I did have another purpose for coming to the library.

The pile of flowers had, if anything, grown slightly. I laid my own down with the rest and stepped back. I felt that I should say something, but I had no idea what. I continued to stand awkwardly for a few moments, increasingly aware of the dubious look from behind the desk.

"Laney…" I began hesitantly. Then words began to come from somewhere. "I read your poems, Laney. Some of them. I'm not much of a reader, actually. But I got it, eventually. I got what you were saying. I heard you." That was all I could think of. I left without looking back.

The rest of the day was spent rereading *Postcards to Myself*. Armed with my new insight I expected to see more in them than I had before – and I wasn't disappointed. There were no more sudden moments of revelation, but now I understood how to look behind the words, each one had a whole new layer of meaning.

"The Chimney", for example. The words were still the same, a vivid description of its old brickwork standing tall amid the devastation of the demolished factory. But behind the description was a feeling of bewildered loneliness. All that had given the chimney purpose was gone. It had been preserved for its architectural significance, but it understood nothing of that. Its world had changed around it, and left it without meaning.

Of course, it wasn't about the chimney at all. Chimneys don't have feelings. But poets do. And this was Laney's voice, speaking about her life, her feelings.

The same sadness was in all the other poems as well. It came through more strongly in some – "The Seagull" was probably the best example, but it pervaded the entire collection. Even "The Party". Although it was funny, there was a hidden sadness. Why was she listening to all these conversations? Because she wasn't having any of her own. Even at a party, she was somehow the one who didn't belong.

It was early evening when I finally drifted back into reality, my mind still swirling with images I had never seen and emotions that weren't my own. But I was cold and cramped from sitting hunched over the keyboard all day. And hungry. I checked the time, and shook my head in amazement. If anyone had told me last week that I would be spending hours at a time reading poetry, I would have told them to get a life.

But now I was hooked, and before I shut down the laptop I downloaded the rest of Laney's books. Also, having become aware of the potential discomfort involved in prolonged reading from a computer, I ordered paperbacks of all three.

I stood up, stretched some of the kinks out, and went into the kitchen to dump something in the microwave. I switched the telly on in passing – it was about time for the local news, and I was wondering if June Henshaw had put out the press release yet.

I was still trying to choose between chicken korma (again) or beef curry when a reporter said a name that got my immediate attention.

My name.

I rushed back into the living room with a frozen ready meal in each hand, and saw my own face staring back at me.

"… named by police as Robert Seaton, of 14 Windsor Road…"

Not just my name and my face, but my address as well.

"… helping the police with their enquiries."

The picture switched to some footage of the high street, zoomed in on bunches of flowers lining the pavement and cable-tied to lampposts. I hadn't been there since it had happened; I hadn't realized the strength of feeling over Laney's death. Finding out like this was a kick in the guts.

The voice-over finished reiterating the story, the announcer moved on to the next item. I became aware that my fingers were becoming uncomfortable, so I dumped the packets back into the freezer and snatched up my phone. Between frozen fingers and a surge of adrenaline it took me a few minutes to find the number Henshaw had given me. That allowed me time to move from shock to anger as it rang unanswered before switching to voicemail.

I swore and tried again. This time it was picked up by a male officer whose name I didn't catch.

"I need to speak to PC Henshaw. Now!"

Police officers don't take kindly to being ordered around by members of the public. There was a distinct frost in his voice as he informed me that PC Henshaw was not available.

"Well, make her available! She promised me anonymity and now my name's been plastered all over the news. Do you know what people have been saying about me already? They're calling me a murderer, and now they know where I live. What the hell's going on!"

Fortunately, the officer was sufficiently professional to pick out the important point in my little rant and not just hang up, as I would have done in his place.

"Sir, I need you to calm down and tell me what your name *is*, please."

I took a deep breath, already feeling embarrassed. Obviously my fame had not yet become so great that any random copper would know at once who I was. "Yes. Of course. Sorry. My name is Robert Seaton, and I've just seen my name and address on the news!"

With a bit more patient probing by the officer, I explained about the accident and the messages on the website; about the press release that Henshaw had promised and what had actually just appeared. The process helped me to get over the initial shock and I found myself agreeing that there was no immediate danger to either my life or my property.

"I'm afraid I don't know what's happened here. I understand your concern, and obviously this needs looking into." The officer, who had introduced himself as PC Baker when I gave him a chance to get a word in, was doing his best to project calm and reason down the line, and it was having some effect, at least in making me feel embarrassed by my panic. "I will send PC Henshaw an email now, and ask her to get in touch with you ASAP. In the meantime, I'll log your call as a 'Concern for Safety' incident so that our control room is informed, and obviously if any threat develops you should call 999 at once."

When he'd hung up, I switched on the laptop and went onto Laney's site. Someone had posted a link to an online local newspaper. My picture again, with the headline "The Man Who Took Our Laney". I switched off again, and sat staring at the blank screen. I might not be in any immediate danger, but I felt like a target.

I wasn't very surprised when my phone rang. With my name and address out there, anyone could find my landline number.

The first caller was some drunk, mumbling incoherent threats and accusations. He sounded so far out of it, I was amazed he'd managed to dial properly. I didn't even try to have a conversation with him.

The next call was more difficult. A woman, sobbing softly, asking me if I understood what I had done. I tried to explain. Several times. But she wasn't listening. She didn't want an explanation, just an excuse to dump her grief onto someone. I hung up on her as well.

The third time it rang, it was a reporter wanting my reaction to the story that had gone out. At last, an opportunity to put my side.

I started to explain that the police had already confirmed it had been an accident, and that I wasn't being charged with anything, but it became clear he wasn't interested in that.

"But how do you feel about it?" he kept asking. "Do you feel guilty? Ashamed?"

I was struggling to understand how I felt myself. Explaining it was way beyond my ability, especially when caught on the hop.

"I'm trying not to feel guilty. Because it wasn't my fault. There was nothing I could do. She just stepped out in front of me. Of course I feel sorry about it. I…"

"So what would you say to her family?"

"What family? I didn't know she had a family."

"Her friends then. All her fans. Have you got anything to say to them?"

"Well, of course I'm desperately sorry, and I understand how much we've lost. She –"

He interrupted again. "Did you know Laney Grey? Have you read her poetry? Are you a fan of hers?"

"No, I never met her, but I have read one of her books and I'm starting to understand what a talented writer she was."

"Do you read a lot of poetry?"

"No, but…"

"How fast were you going?"

"What?" The sudden change of subject caught me by surprise.

"When you hit her. How fast were you going?"

"About forty. The speed limit."

"About. So you're not sure. How long have you been driving? Had you driven that vehicle before? Are you familiar with that stretch of road?"

I had had more than enough by now. "Yes, I am sure, and I'm an experienced –"

He interrupted again. "Had you been drinking, Mr Seaton? Or were you on something? Did you take any medication that day?"

DAY 4: OFFICE WORK

"No, I didn't!" I shouted down the phone, and hung up.

It rang again almost immediately. I stared at it, but the ringing went on until I pulled the wire out. I barely restrained myself from smashing the thing into the wall then stomping the remains into the carpet. I'd seen people do that on TV, and thought it was a bit over the top. I understood now. The adrenaline rush made me desperate for physical action. I wanted to deal with my fear and anger by breaking something.

Instead I sat with my head in my hands and concentrated on calming down; not thinking about anything but the air moving in and out of my lungs. It began to work. My heartbeat slowed, my breathing steadied.

My mobile rang. I snatched it up and stared at the screen. Unknown number. Not many people had my mobile number. Colin had it at work for emergencies. A few mates, a couple of girls I'd dated and who'd never used it.

I accepted the call, while promising myself that if this was about PPI they were going to get an earful that would put them off cold-calling for evermore.

"Hello? Mr Seaton? Ray Colshaw, from *The Echo*. I'd just like to ask you –"

"How did you get this number?" I interrupted.

There was a pause. "Mr Seaton, did you know Laney Grey at all?"

I cut the connection and switched off the phone. Colshaw didn't need to answer my question, because I'd remembered who else I'd given the number to.

I'd given it to June Henshaw. The police had had my mobile number.

37

DAY 5: COMPLICATIONS

I didn't sleep well that night. My flat was on the top floor at the rear of a converted three-storey town house, and I rarely heard any noise from the street. But with my nerves screwed tight, the smallest sound was enough to accelerate my heart and send me to my window – even though there was nothing to be seen except an overgrown patch of grass.

Sometime in the small hours, I finally dozed off, only to be woken a few hours later by heavy knocking on the door, accompanied by an authoritative voice calling my name. Bleary-eyed, I pulled on a pair of joggers and stumbled over to open it.

The two coppers there were bad enough, but they were accompanied by my landlord, which made it serious.

"PC Barnes, PC Asadi. We just needed to check that you're OK, Mr Seaton. Only there's been an incident."

"An incident?"

"Someone's sprayed 'MURDERER' across Mrs Fletcher's windows," said the landlord, a rotund man with a permanent frown. "In green paint!"

I wasn't sure what the colour had to do with it, but Mrs Fletcher was an elderly widow who had the front ground floor flat.

"She's very upset," he continued. "And it's all down to you, you know."

"If you don't mind, Mr Johnson?" PC Barnes intervened.

"We're not suggesting that you're responsible, Mr Seaton. But it does seem likely to be connected to recent events."

I gave him a stony look. "Such as the police giving out my address and telephone number?"

"I don't know anything about that, sir. Our first concern is your safety. Did you see or hear anything overnight?"

I shook my head. "No. Nothing since I disconnected my phone." I told them about the calls I'd had.

"We'll be treating this as criminal damage at present," Barnes said to me and the landlord. "We'll get some photographs of the graffiti, and the paint spray can we found outside – green paint – that'll go off to the forensics lab. Might be some prints on it. Obviously, if there are any further incidents, or any more threats, Mr Seaton, call us."

The other copper, PC Asadi, had stepped out of the room and was talking on his radio. "Mr Seaton?" he called through the door. "PC Henshaw just called me up. She's at the station and she's been trying to contact you."

I went over to the phone socket, plugged it back in, and checked for a tone. "Tell her to try again," I told him.

The phone rang almost at once. I answered it warily, but it was her voice.

"Let me say straight off, the press release that went out is not the one I sent."

"So what went wrong, then?" I caught my landlord's eye as I spoke, and nodded meaningfully at the door. He didn't look happy about leaving, but Barnes politely escorted him out and shut the door behind them.

"I've been trying to find out myself," she said. "I didn't see the news last night, so I didn't know anything about it till this morning. I called the Press Office as soon as I got in, but they don't start till nine."

I glanced at the clock and was mildly surprised to see that it was only just eight. "OK, but what are you going to do about it?

Have you heard what happened here last night?"

"Yes. I'm looking at the incident log now."

"There's people running round out there thinking I'm a murderer! What's going to happen next? A petrol bomb through the window?"

"That's not very likely. A drunk with a spray can is a long way from arson. And we are aware of the situation. If anything kicks off, dial three nines and we'll be there on blues and twos. In the meantime, just sit tight. I'll get back to you as soon as I can find out something. Keep your phone on."

"No. Forget that. I don't want any more hassle from reporters. Hold on a moment…" I put the phone down and had a quick rummage through some drawers, coming up with an old (pre-smartphone) mobile. "Use this number," I told her. "But don't give it to anyone else."

"Understood. I'll speak to you later."

She hung up, and I went back to searching drawers, hoping to find a compatible charger. Something I really should have thought of before I made plans to use the phone.

I'd just found one (and was trying to remember how to put the SIM card back without wrecking it) when there was another knock on the door and Johnson walked back in, without the coppers and without waiting for an invitation.

"Mrs Fletcher is very upset," he announced.

"I expect she is," I agreed. "I'm not ecstatic about things myself."

He glared at me, and I met his gaze, daring him to say what was there in his eyes. Daring him to come right out with it.

Daring him to say it was my fault.

Instead he looked away. "Never had anything like this at my property before. Police coming round, paint on the windows." He glared again. "And it wasn't even your window!"

"Well, if you'd installed a separate intercom to each flat – as you promised to do six months ago – they would have used that to hassle me, instead of graffiti!"

DAY 5: COMPLICATIONS

His frown became even more pronounced. "Don't try and make this about me. All I'm saying is that I can't have all the residents being upset over this. And it's not like that paint's easy to get rid of. Some of it went on the brickwork, and you can't just sponge that off, you know. It'll need specialist cleaning, and that doesn't come cheap."

I nodded, recognizing that we had finally got to his real area of concern. "Would it help if I paid for the cleaning?"

His frown eased a little. "I think that's the least you can do."

I shook my head. "No, the least I could do would be to allow you to fulfil your obligations as landlord and sort it out yourself. This is going well beyond the least I can do, and I'm only doing it out of consideration for the other residents, who would otherwise be left waiting weeks until you got round to sorting it out – and probably doing a second-rate job of it then!"

And besides that, I didn't want my home marked out with the word "MURDERER" in large green letters.

His frown came back full strength, but I continued before he could get another word out. "I'll get on to it today. Right now, in fact – so if you wouldn't mind?" I nodded towards the door, and he began a reluctant retreat in that direction.

"I hope that's the last of it," he said on the way out. "If there are any more of these incidents, I may have to give you notice."

"That's OK. I was thinking of leaving anyway."

Johnson gave an indignant snort, turned his back, and swept out in a landlordly fashion. The effect was somewhat diminished when he stumbled on a loose bit of lino on the landing.

"That needs fixing as well," I called after him. "I have told you about it."

He scurried off without reply.

I shut the door firmly behind him and turned to survey the room, wondering if I really would have to leave. I'd been here five years, or thereabouts. It was convenient for work, and there were two pubs, three takeaways, and a supermarket within walking distance. The ideal bachelor pad, in fact. Comfortable. Perhaps a bit untidy, but comfortable.

The jacket tossed across the chair, that was comfortable. The grubby T-shirt crumpled up on the sofa – that was comfortable. Perhaps pushing the boundaries a bit. The sofa itself, like the rest of the furniture, had come with the flat. It had probably been quite smart in its day, but white leather doesn't fare well in a bachelor environment. The cigarette burns on the arms had been left by a previous tenant – hadn't I meant to get a throw or something to cover those up? – but the coffee stains were all mine.

I wandered into the tiny kitchen area and contemplated the sink full of washing-up awaiting attention. Perhaps more than a bit untidy. I found myself wondering what Laney would have thought of it. Would it have inspired a poem? My imagination projected a holographic Laney into the middle of my poky little living room, smiling sadly as she looked around her. And in a sudden moment of painful clarity, I realized what sort of poem she would have written.

Nothing about the place itself. Laney's talent was to look past the superficial, below the surface. She'd have seen what the flat implied; what it said about the occupant. If she'd seen the flat, she'd have written about me. And I didn't care to think about what she might have said.

"Leave me alone!" I muttered. "You stepped out in front of me, and look at all the trouble that's come my way since. I don't need you getting all judgmental." I shook my head, deleting the mental image of her. But the flat was still a tip. Well, I didn't have a lot else to do. I finished setting up the phone, left it on charge, and started cleaning up.

June Henshaw called back while I was still halfway through the washing-up.

"So have you sorted out what happened with the press release?" I asked.

"I am instructed to inform you that the matter is being looked into." Her tone was strange, a sort of formal stoniness that did not allow for argument or appeal. It wasn't what I'd become accustomed to hearing from her.

"I am further instructed to inform you that the fatal RTC that you were involved with is now being dealt with by the Criminal Investigation Department. If you have any queries to make, or any further information to offer, you should contact Detective Constable Cadenti at this police station."

"Cadenti? Is that the same one who came to see me before?"

"Yes, Mr Seaton. That is correct."

"Well… when will I hear any more about this?"

"You will be contacted if there are any developments. Goodbye, Mr Seaton." She hung up, leaving me bewildered and not at all happy. Something had happened to cause this change of attitude, but it didn't seem likely that I was going to find out what.

I was still thinking that through when the mobile rang again. A different number, not one I recognized. Another reporter? Had my new contact details been leaked already – in spite of Henshaw's promise to keep them to herself? After the last conversation, I wasn't sure how much I could trust her. Warily, I accepted the call, ready to hang up if I didn't like what I heard.

"Mr Seaton?" Her voice. But it sounded more natural this time. "I'm sorry about that last call. I know it must have sounded really bad. But I didn't have much choice. I had DS Fayden and his tame DI standing over me to make sure I kept to the script. His script."

"I didn't think it sounded right. I take it you're free to talk now?"

"I'm on my mobile, in the ladies' loo. Should be OK for a while."

"So what the… heck's going on?"

There was a pause. "It's too complicated to explain over the phone. Do you know The Stag, in Anniston?"

Anniston was about fifteen miles away. It was on one of our delivery routes, and I vaguely recalled seeing a sprawling modern pub on the way in. "On the main road? Just off a big roundabout? I've never been in there."

"Neither have I. That's the point. We're not likely to be recognized. Can you be there at eight tonight?"

"Yes, OK."

"I'll see you in the bar, then."

"Right. I'll get the drinks in, shall I?"

"It's not a date," she said sharply, and hung up.

That left me a day to get through without going out. I wasn't keen on the possibility of meeting whoever had painted "MURDERER" on the house. Or any reporters, either.

I finished cleaning and tidying up the flat, I found a company that would clean paint off brickwork, and I called Colin and told him that I wouldn't be going in that day. He, it turned out, had been trying to get hold of me to tell me not to go in.

"We've been infested with reporters all day," he said. "On the phone and in person. They want to know all about you, of course, but they're asking about the company as well. Wanting to know if our drivers are properly trained; if we have a policy on drugs and alcohol; if you're facing any disciplinary action."

"What did you tell them?"

"I told them that you are an exemplary driver, that our training and our policies on drugs and alcohol match or exceed all relevant guidelines, and that there is no question of any disciplinary action, since you were not at fault in any way."

"Oh. Thanks."

"No more than the truth, Rob. But, having said that, it might be better if you stayed off for a few days. If they get word that you're around, they might come back."

"OK. I need to get my car, though. It's parked in the yard."

"Do you still keep the spare keys in your locker?"

"Yes. Key ring with a Mickey Mouse fob."

"Right. Well, I'll bring it round to you myself; save you coming over. If you're happy with that?"

44

DAY 5: COMPLICATIONS

I agreed, reflecting that I was learning about the power of the press. Without having done anything at all I was now barred from my work and threatened with eviction.

Colin might almost have heard my thoughts. "Don't worry. This will soon blow over. Reporters have a short attention span."

Which left me wondering just how much media attention was needed to wreck someone's life.

With the day starting to drag, I went back to Laney's poems. I was still wondering about that "black gull". Having drawn a blank in her first book, I decided to try the next one. *Stepping out of Shadow*, it was called. It had been published less than a year after *Postcards to Myself*. I wondered at that. Nothing at all for years, then a sudden burst of creativity. What had the trigger been?

I scanned the contents page, didn't see anything obviously seagull flavoured, skipped the intro, and scrolled through to the first poem. "Dancer", it was called, and it was about a leaf. An autumn leaf, dead and brown on its branch until the wind stroked it and stirred it and wrenched it free to go spinning and swirling and dancing away. Up into the sky and off into the distance. Finally a little black speck, then gone from sight.

Before I'd finished reading, I knew that something had changed.

It was very much Laney in style, with the same intensity of description that I had first seen – and been puzzled by – in "The Wave". And having learned how to look beyond the words for the meaning, I knew at once that this was about her. But it was a different Laney. The sadness, the loneliness that had pervaded her first book had vanished. The sense of isolation, of never being really part of life, was gone. Instead there was an overwhelming exuberance. An explosion of uninhibited joy. She was the leaf, broken free from her old life and dancing with the wind.

Of course, the leaf wouldn't dance forever. Sooner or later, the wind would abandon it, drop it, let it float to the ground to rot. But the leaf didn't look ahead, and neither did she. When she wrote the poem, she was entirely given over to the dance, living totally in the moment.

"What happened?" I asked her. "What changed for you, Laney?"

Something significant, and something pretty good. As I read on, the same theme was repeated. Laney saw her new joy, her freedom, reflected everywhere. At a football match, for example. Just a small local affair, but as she described it, the jubilation (her word!) when the home team scored was enough to fill Wembley.

But there was something else there as well. Something else new.

I didn't see it at first. But then I noticed a word I couldn't remember Laney using before.

"We".

Talking about the tension, the almost painful hope the fans felt as the home side attacked, driving the ball forward towards the goal, she said "we". She included herself in the crowd. She was no longer standing apart, watching. She was involved.

The difference in her between the first book and the second was huge. I began to rush through the rest of the collection, looking for clues. Looking for what had caused the change.

I found it in the last poem of the collection, "Walking the Street". Unlike most of Laney's work, this was unambiguously about her. Even "The Goal" hadn't been so clear in this. But here she was reliving an experience she'd actually had. She had walked down that street, and almost every step had triggered memories. Starting with the battered street sign, where "Willdyne Street" (a tribute to some long-forgotten local prominence) had been altered to read "Willy Street". Just as it had been when she played here with other children.

Outside the corner shop – now closed – she recalled the crates of fruit and vegetables that had surrounded the door, the dim clutter of tins and boxes within, the jars of sweets, the heft and excitement of a quarter of wine gums.

From that open window had come strains of violin music,

incongruous and memorable when Radio One blared from other houses.

This doorway still bore traces of the bright red paint she had watched being applied, though it had now faded to dull pink. Another house evoked the smell of baking bread, and in a bay window she looked, unsuccessfully, for the fat ginger cat that had stared suspiciously back at her.

It took a while to reach her destination: number 15, halfway down on the right, blue door, brass door furniture. The final line explained everything.

> I put a finger on the doorbell
> Hesitated, feeling the action misplaced.
> Then, smiling to myself, I put out a hand
> And touched smooth brass that welcomed
>   my fingers.
> I turned the door knob, pushed,
> And went home.

That was it. Her joy, her new sense of belonging, her dancing with the wind, came down to this: she had come home. I sat for a while, not so much thinking about that as absorbing the emotion of it.

A knock on the door dragged me rudely back from Laney's world to my own. It was Colin, dropping off my car keys.

"It's parked in the next street," he said. "I would have left it outside, but I think you've got reporters."

"What? Outside?"

"Across the street in a car. There was someone pointing a camera at the front door when I drove past, so I kept going. Doesn't matter if they see me – they already know who I am – but I thought you might not want them to know your car."

I nodded. "Good thinking. Thanks, Colin."

"Especially considering what they've already been saying about you."

47

"They've... what? What have they said?"

Colin pulled a folded newspaper out of his pocket and handed it over with a sad shake of his head. "This morning's edition of the local rag."

I unfolded it warily. The front page was dominated by a picture of the accident scene, with a huge mound of flowers half covering the pavement. A fuzzy black and white picture of me was inset. But it was the headline that caught my attention and kicked me in the guts. Harsh black capitals shouting at me: "KILLER DRIVER FEELS NO GUILT".

"But that's not true!" I protested. "That's not what I said. Not what I meant."

Colin shrugged. "Of course not. I didn't believe it. But newspapers will say anything to sell a few copies. This one will, at any rate."

I quickly scanned through the rest of the article. I could barely recognize the bare bones of the telephone interview under the pile of speculation, insinuation, and character assassination that made up most of the piece.

"How the hell can they get away with it?" I sat down, feeling slightly sick. "Can't I sue them or something?"

Colin shrugged. "It depends. Have they printed anything which is factually untrue? Or quoted you inaccurately?"

I shook my head. "It's more about how they interpreted it."

"Then I doubt you've got a case. And even if you did, it'd be long, expensive, and the best result you could get would be a short apology buried in the back pages. In the meantime, they'd love the extra publicity."

"What am I supposed to do then? Anyone who reads this will think I'm an insensitive scumbag who can run someone down and walk away laughing about it."

Colin came and sat down next to me. "Nobody who knows you will think that. And this time next week nobody's going to remember it anyway." He forced a laugh. "Who the heck reads local newspapers anyway? Trust me, Rob – keep your head down, stay off their radar, and this whole thing will soon blow over." He gave me what was presumably meant to be a reassuring, bloke-to-bloke punch on the shoulder. Coming from Colin, it was awkward and a bit scary. But I understood the intention.

"Thanks. I hope you're right."

"I am." He stood up to leave. "Might be an idea to go away for a few days. Change of scenery, take your mind off it."

"Might be a good idea. I'll think about it."

"You do that. Keep in touch, though." He stepped out of the door, then glanced back in. "Oh, by the way, you've got a brake light out." He gave a little half-wave and shut the door behind him.

Brake light. Great. Just what I needed to hear before I went to meet a copper.

My flat didn't have any windows overlooking the street, but there was one at the end of the communal landing. Peering out from behind the grimy net curtain, I saw a sporty red Corsa parked opposite. I'd no idea what reporters normally drove, but I was pretty sure that I hadn't seen it on the street before. From this angle, I couldn't see if anyone was in it or not, but I was happy to take Colin's word for that. And I fully agreed with him that I didn't want them knowing my car. And suppose they followed me; saw me meeting with June Henshaw? I shuddered to think what headlines they might make out of that. But how was I going to get out without being seen? The front door was the only exit.

I went back to my flat and stared down at the walled-in patch of rough grass and mud that was loosely termed "the back garden". Open for the use of all residents – though the only use anyone made of it was to dump rubbish. I could see a broken TV, two washing machines, and a rotting mattress, plus various smaller items. The walls were six foot high and solid. There was no way out there.

At least, not officially.

On the other side of the wall was a slightly better-kept garden, with less mud, more grass, and no rubbish. It belonged to a terraced house nearly identical to the one my flat was in. Shortly after I'd moved in, it had been broken into – through the back door. The police had concluded that the burglar had made his way there by climbing over the walls. Or running along the tops of them. A dangerous route, especially at night, but it seemed he'd been pretty confident – he'd tried several houses before finding one left conveniently unlocked.

Where someone could get in, I could get out.

I checked my watch. It was nearly half past four. At this time of year it would be getting dark by six thirty. To make my appointment (not a date) with June in good time I'd need to leave by seven.

I opened the window and leaned out. The dividing wall continued all the way to the end of the row, where it met the cross street on which Colin had left my car. It looked the same all the way: flat-topped brick, about six inches wide. No obvious changes in height, no visible obstacles. It looked easy enough. Anyone could walk a straight six-inch line, couldn't they? Well, anyone sober, and I wasn't planning to start drinking.

I glanced up at the sky. The spell of warm, dry weather that we'd had since the accident was breaking, and the sky was sullen with low grey clouds. Showers were forecast. Rain might make the brick slippery. Falling off a wall that high could break something. Possibly my neck.

Still thinking it over, I showered and tried to find something appropriate to wear for a non-date with a police officer. My cleaning frenzy revealed that I owned a lot of T-shirts and several pairs of jeans (mostly worn, torn, or just grubby), but not much in the category of "smart", or even "smart very casual". Eventually I unearthed a reasonable shirt, a tie that almost matched, and a crumpled pair of cords. With my black leather jacket and a cleaned-up pair of trainers, I was fit for decent society. Or at least for The Stag.

DAY 5: COMPLICATIONS

Time wore on. The clouds hung ever lower, and began a steady drizzle. It was going to get dark early. I went back out to the landing and checked on the Corsa. Still there. Surely it wouldn't stay all night? But if I was going to try the wall, it would be better done while there was some light.

I'd found a torch earlier. I flicked the button and got a dim glow. A further search produced some batteries, but they were completely dead.

The clock crept past six. The Corsa remained in place, the rain continued, the light faded further.

I went down to the back garden, and dragged one of the dead washing machines across to the far corner. Climbing up would be easy, and it was only five houses along to the end.

I stood on the washing machine, which creaked and wobbled but held my weight.

I scrambled up on the wall, and stood carefully. It was remarkable how narrow six inches looked when that was all there was to stand on. There wasn't much light left to see where I was putting my feet. On the other hand, there was quite enough light for anyone looking out to see me. And how was I going to explain that? "Oh, good evening; just out for a stroll."

Why would anyone look out? I asked myself. *It's not like there's a view.*

I started walking. The top of the wall had been finished off with a thin skim of cement. It was slick and slippery in the rain. In some places it was crumbling away. I walked as quickly as I dared, arms outstretched for balance.

Two houses along. I was starting to gain some confidence, moving a little faster, with the far end of the wall in sight.

"Eeeeeee! HAROLD! HAROLD!"

The shriek came from my left, and I jumped. Literally. My tense nerves sent wild panic signals to my muscles, and I leaped a foot into the air. Not a good thing to do when you're standing on top of a wall – and a wet, crumbly wall at that. I didn't help things by simultaneously trying to turn to see where the scream had come from.

Coming down again, one foot missed the wall entirely. The other came down half on the brickwork. Something crumbled under the impact, and I was falling backwards. There were no lights on this side of the wall, and I fell into thick shadow. I could have landed on hard concrete or worse. Instead, I crashed into thick bushes, which only knocked the wind out of me.

I lay gasping for breath as quietly as I could while the conversation continued on the other side of the wall.

"There was a man, Harold. Walking along the wall like he was strolling down the pavement!"

"Well, there's nothing there now." A man's voice, sounding irritated. "Probably a cat."

"I know a cat when I see one, Harold, and cats don't walk along walls on their hind legs!"

They don't fall off and nearly break their back, either, I thought to myself.

"I think you should call the police," the woman continued, and I nearly shouted "No, don't!" in panic. It was, in a way, fortunate that I was still trying to get my breath back and could only manage a faint croak.

"Call the police?" Harold was saying. "And what am I supposed to tell them? My wife's seen a cat walking on its hind legs? Get them out searching for Puss-in-Boots?"

"They'll be out searching for a missing husband if you don't watch yourself!" A window slammed shut, leaving me alone in my bush.

When I was breathing again, I began the slow process of freeing myself without scratching my eyes out on the way. It helped when I was able to get my phone out of my pocket. It wasn't sophisticated enough to have a torch, but the light of the screen was enough to show me that I hadn't fallen into a hawthorn hedge as I'd feared, but a scraggly bit of privet. A few minutes of careful moving and quiet swearing and I was standing on the green, green grass of someone's back garden.

The house was in darkness. I wasn't sure if that was good or bad. If the place was locked up and empty, I'd be spared having to explain my presence. On the other hand, I might be trapped here. Even if I wanted to risk the wall again, I wasn't sure if I could get back onto it. There were no dead washing machines here to give me a helpful step up.

I approached the door and gave it a hesitant knock, mentally rehearsing what I could say. *Sorry to bother you, but I was just out for a stroll and I happened to fall into your back garden.* Somehow, I couldn't make it sound convincing. It was almost a relief when no one answered.

I knocked again, a little louder. Still no response.

Taking a deep breath, I tried the door handle. It turned. Stiffly, but it turned, and when I pushed on the door it creaked open.

I was staring into a dark room. A kitchen. My phone showed a sink, full of dirty plates, a gas cooker, cupboards – a doorway. I could hear voices beyond, too faint to make out the words, but a man and a woman were talking.

I wet my lips and prepared to announce myself, but the conversation was interrupted by a sudden burst of machine-gun fire.

The TV was on, I realized, as I picked myself up from the floor where my overstretched nerves had sent me. Dramatic background music was the clue.

I crept closer to the door, which was just ajar, and eased it open. Beyond was a dimly lit hallway, with doors on the right and at the far end. The end door had a letterbox in it.

Opening the kitchen door a bit more, I stepped into the hallway. The creak of a floorboard underfoot was mostly drowned out by a well-timed explosion, and I made my way towards the front door to the sounds of battle and tension-inducing music. I was glad of the noise to cover the sound of creaking floorboards, but I didn't need any more tension. Knowing that the door could open at any moment – and that there wasn't the slightest hope of coming up with an excuse for my presence – was giving me plenty of that.

I crept past the side doors. The front door was just a few steps away. I could now see that the poor security at the back of the house was more than compensated for at the front. There were two bolts, a chain, and a Yale. Plus a good old-fashioned mortise lock, with no sign of a key.

As I reached the door, peace inconveniently broke out on the TV, with a consequent drop in the noise level. I was suddenly very aware of my heart, thumping like a piledriver on speed. I stood absolutely still, not daring to move for fear of the noise being heard.

There was music again. Closing credits, perhaps. And what happens when the film finishes? Go to the kitchen and make a cup of tea maybe?

I grabbed at the bolts, torn between the opposing needs of silence and speed. The top one slid open easily; the bottom one was stiff, and squeaked as I wrenched it open. The chain came off without trouble, but where was the key for the main lock? Not hanging by the door, as was often the case. Not on top of the cupboard by the door. Perhaps in the cupboard? I tugged at the handle; it stuck, and the entire cupboard rocked forward. Something inside it fell with a thump.

The music on the TV faded to an announcer. I twisted on the Yale, pushed desperately on the door. Then pulled, and it swung easily open, the mortise lock not even engaged. I fell over backwards, landing hard and painfully on the thin carpet, but adrenaline bounced me back to my feet and shot me out of the door before it had stopped swinging.

I was nearly at the end of the street before I had the presence of mind to go back and shut the door. There was a lit window next to it. Peering through a gap in the blind, I could see the TV. In front of it an elderly couple sat together on a sofa, hand in hand and both apparently sound asleep.

DAY 5: COMPLICATIONS

I found my car exactly where Colin had said, and (after a brief moment of panic when I couldn't find my keys) got in and started the engine.

Then I sat behind the wheel and shook uncontrollably for several minutes. Reaction, of course. That was all. Tightly wound nerves relaxing. Quite natural.

But another part of myself was stepping back, taking a look, and shaking its head. Wondering what the hell had happened to me. Where was the relaxed, happy, confident Rob – the one with the normal life? Who was this nervous wreck of a bloke, having ridiculous adventures, being pursued by the press like a wayward celebrity, having secret meetings with the police, and reading poetry? What had Laney Grey done to me?

There was no answer to that question. Not yet, anyway.

I took a backstreet route, avoiding the front of my house in case my stalker recognized me as I drove by. Also in case he had given up and gone home while I was playing burglar, which I'd rather not know about.

I'd missed the worst of the rush hour, and made good time to Anniston. Driving was easier now than when I'd made the Fiesta run; I still felt nervous, but without the extreme tension that had nearly paralysed me before. I was in The Stag by quarter past seven, trying to make myself presentable in the gents. The mud and blood mostly wiped off, but I couldn't do much about the scratches on my face or the massive rip in my trousers. On the positive side, it could have been worse: the left leg was torn right up to the knee, but at least nothing embarrassing was revealed.

However, the overall effect wasn't impressive. *Just as well it's not a date*, I thought gloomily as I walked to the bar.

After the day I'd had, a serious drink would have been welcome. But I was driving, and meeting a copper, so when June walked in I was sipping on a cappuccino.

It would have been an exaggeration to say I nearly didn't

recognize her, but she did look very different out of uniform. She was wearing jeans and a pink woolly top. Without the bulky stab vest she looked less stocky, and her pale blonde hair was down, giving her face a gentler look.

"Hi. You're looking nice," I said. Speaking without thinking, as usual.

The smile that she had been forming faded into a frown. "You don't. You look like you were dragged through a hedge! What happened?"

I shook my head. "I fell over. Long story."

She raised an eyebrow. Just because she was out of uniform, it didn't mean that her police instincts were suppressed.

"I had to take an alternative route out. There's a reporter watching my flat; I didn't want to be seen leaving."

"A reporter?" She seemed sceptical.

"Yes. I think so. They've been after me non-stop since they got hold of my address. That's why I had to change my number. You should see what they've written about me."

"I did. You shouldn't have talked to the press at all. Anything you said was going to get used against you."

"But I didn't know…"

She waved aside my protest. "I can't see them sitting around watching the flat. We're talking about the local rag here, not the international paparazzi. They don't have that many people to spare. And to be honest, you're not that important."

Her assessment was unnecessarily harsh, I thought. "Well, someone's been watching my front door all day."

"Have you seen them?"

"Yes! Well, I've seen their car, and it doesn't belong on our street. And Colin – my boss – saw them pointing a camera."

"A camera?" June's eyes narrowed. "OK, that could be suspicious. What sort of car was it?"

"New model Corsa. Sporty looking, red with flash silver stripes down the side?"

"And a ridiculously large spoiler on the back? Looks like it was nicked off a Formula One race car?"

"Yes, that's it! Do you know it?"

She looked reluctant, but nodded. "I think so. It sounds like Andy Hart's ride."

"Andy Hart? Who's he? Some sort of freelance reporter?"

"No. He's a copper. A keen young PC with more ambition than intelligence."

My jaw dropped. "You mean I'm being watched by the police!"

My voice rose with the shock, and June shushed me frantically. "Keep it down, for f... goodness' sake!"

"Sorry, but what are you saying here? I'm under surveillance by... your lot?"

"Not exactly, no." She glanced around. The bar area was quite busy, with people coming for drinks, waiting for drinks, and leaving with drinks in a steady stream of alcohol. "See if you can find us a quiet spot to talk in. I'm going to get a drink."

"OK. It's Rob, by the way."

"Yes. I know. Call me June."

I managed to get us a table for two stuck in a far corner with a nice view of the kitchen. June joined me, clasping a large red wine. She noticed me noticing it.

"It's been a long day and I know my limit, OK? Ignore it and I won't ask about your fall."

I shrugged. "Fair enough. I've ordered something. I know it's not a date, but they won't let you have a table unless you're eating."

"Right."

"So what were you saying about this copper who's watching my door?"

"I'll get to that." She took a healthy sip of her wine, set it down. "First off, though, you've got to understand something. Just by meeting here with you, I'm putting my career on the line. At the very least. And that's before I even tell you anything. Once I start giving you information about an active police investigation, then

57

I'm breaking the law. So if it ever comes out, then I'm seriously screwed."

"I see why you needed the wine."

She grinned. "Just to make it clear, you'd be equally screwed. Obtaining confidential information from a police officer? Not taken lightly, I promise!"

"OK, I get the picture. I keep it hush. But why take the risk, June?"

"Sometimes doing the right thing means breaking the rules. And I am not best pleased with Mickey Fayden. This time he's gone way over the top."

A waitress came over with a very large plate. June stopped talking and sat back as it was placed between us. It didn't leave much space on the table.

She raised an eyebrow. "Quick service! But what's this?"

"This is the Super Sharer Stag Platter. I didn't know what you liked, but this seems to have a bit of everything. Bready things, fishy things, meaty things, and… thingy things. Everything except actual stag, in fact. And I know it's still not a date, but it's on me."

"Bribing a police officer now?" She said it sharply, but with a smile.

"Gesture of appreciation. A bit of a thank you."

"I've had a long day, didn't get off shift until late and then came straight here. So the gesture is accepted, and thank you too." She selected a garlic breadstick, swirled it in a dip, and munched. "Have you ever heard of Lappies?"

I was trying out a breaded mushroom with sweet chilli, and shook my head.

"Chill Pills? Coolers? Spanish Bliss?"

"Never heard of them."

"I'm glad to hear it. They're all street names for a new type of designer drug. There's not a lot of intel on it, but the word is that it was developed in a legitimate pharmaceutical lab, as a stress reliever. The product didn't meet the requirements, and it was never licensed for commercial use. However, someone must have seen some potential in it, and nicked the formula. A few months after the project was officially discontinued, the stuff started showing up in Spain, where it was known as 'La Paz'. 'The Peace', in English – or Lappies."

"OK, so it's a stolen formula. But what's the big deal about a stress buster?"

"Oh, this is more than just a stress buster. La Paz is a total emotion suppressor. A dose of this and you don't feel anything. No worry, no fear, no anger. You can still think quite clearly, but any emotional content is gone."

I thought about it. "That's a bit weird, but it doesn't sound too bad."

"I know. That was my first thought as well. But the thing is, once you take out the emotions, you also take out inhibitions. It's emotions that stop people from doing a lot of things. Fear of consequences, concern for others, and so on."

She paused to take a long sip of wine. "Alcohol does that a bit," she said, looking thoughtfully into her glass. "That's why people wake up in cells thinking, 'Oh heck. Why did I do that?' But Lappies take it a whole lot further.

"The first definite case involving this new poison was in Madrid. A teenager was trying to walk along the railing on a bridge, missed, and went down fifty feet to hard concrete. The kids with him said that he wasn't scared at all. Even when he fell, he didn't scream."

"Nasty." I thought of what a long drop might do to a fragile human body, and winced.

"There were a few others like that. Then the first murder. A young woman stabbed her mother with a kitchen knife. Not in a moment of anger, as most of these domestic crimes are. She wanted money, her mother refused to give it her. So she went into the kitchen, got a carving knife and stabbed her mother through the neck while she was watching TV. Afterwards, when the drug wore off, she went crazy with grief. She loved her mother. But she hadn't felt it when La Paz was at work in her. She acted without any feeling at all."

I put down a spicy battered sausage, my appetite suddenly reduced. "That's... terrible. Beyond terrible."

June gave me a sombre look. "It gets worse. The original, lab version wasn't addictive. But someone messed with it. Mixed it with something, made it so addictive that one dose was enough to get you hooked. The girl killed her mother to get money for another hit."

I said nothing. Stories like that belonged in TV dramas or news reports. Stories that weren't real, or whose reality was kept at a safe distance by the screen. They shouldn't be told in a matter-of-fact way across the table.

June sipped her wine before continuing. "The stuff began turning up all over Spain, spilled across the borders into Portugal and the south of France. It was particularly popular among petty criminals – burglars and such like. Kept them calm and focused while they were about their business. But the pushers were opening up other markets as well. Students, even schoolkids. Helped them study or cope with exam nerves. Respectable business people, professionals, politicians – anyone who might be stressed or under pressure. Ironic really, since that was the original target group for the drug."

"Were there any more deaths?"

"Oh yes. Eight murders, five suicides, and a dozen other incidents linked to La Paz in a twelve-month period. That's the ones that were confirmed. The Spanish police put a lot of resources into tracking down the people behind it, but it was a tough one to crack. The dealers weren't using the usual distribution vectors – the bars and nightclubs, and cars parked on dark streets. They were finding ways to get directly into the schools and universities, into businesses and community centres. Typically, they'd identify someone with good access and get them hooked."

"How long did it go on for?"

60

"Over a year. Then they tracked down the source. Closed down production, picked up most of the people involved."

I raised an eyebrow. "Most?"

"Somebody got away. One of the main people. Disappeared completely, and didn't leave behind so much as a description. There's a suspicion that he had a contact in the police who tipped him off, but it was never proved."

June leaned back in her chair and finished her wine. "There were no clues about this person. Nobody who had been arrested had ever met him; he always worked at a distance. He ran the business by text, mostly. But La Paz was off the streets and the source destroyed, so it seemed like game over. Until a few months ago. Then it turned up again. Here."

"Here in the UK?"

"Here in this part of the UK." She glanced down at the Super Sharer Stag Platter, now reduced to a few crumbs. "That was a pretty impressive starter."

"Do you want a main?" I felt I had to ask.

"No, but I wouldn't say no to a sweet." She grinned. "If you're still paying?"

For a non-date, this was turning out to be more expensive than some of my actual dates. Of course, it had lasted longer than most of them.

"Of course." I returned the grin. "But I'll skip if you don't mind."

"No problem. You can watch me enjoy mine."

Several minutes later, over a large slice of honeycomb cheesecake, she resumed. "To understand what's going on here, you have to understand Mickey Fayden."

"That's the detective sergeant who came with all the questions, right?"

She nodded.

"I got the impression that you didn't much like him."

June laughed at that. A cynical and world-weary laugh that

pretty much confirmed what I'd thought. "Me and Mickey have some history. We went through training together. He was convinced that he was there as a special favour to the force, and while he was waiting for them to recognize that and make him chief constable, he would favour me with his attention – because after all, he was also God's gift to women. I told him to get lost, and called him a loser. Now, Mickey doesn't take rejection well, and he got a bit pushy about it. I pushed back, and broke his wrist. That could have ended his career right there. Perhaps mine as well though, so officially he slipped in the shower. But skip on a few years, and I'm still a PC, while he's a DS, the rising star of CID. He takes every opportunity to rub my nose in it. 'Not doing bad for a loser, eh?' he tells me every time we meet. I think that the label hurt him worse than the wrist."

"OK. But what's that got to do with…"

She held up a hand. "I'm getting to it, all right? So, here's Mickey Fayden, desperately ambitious, made it to DS but wants to move up to DI – detective inspector – as fast as he can. And he hears this rumour about a new drug on the street."

"La Paz?"

She nodded. "Or Lappies, in the local speak. Now, Mickey has also heard something else of interest. About someone with a few question marks about their past history who's just moved into town. Moved in from Spain, as it happens. Had a bit of cash on him as well. Enough to buy a run-down old pub near the city centre and have it completely refurbished.

"Now, to all appearances the new boy in town, who goes by the name of Mateo Canoso, is a perfectly legitimate businessman. He's in the country legally, he's investing in the community, he's making friends in useful places. But the pub he's done up used to have a bit of a reputation. The sort of place where you could get something a bit stronger than alcohol. And there's a whisper on the street that the new-look King William has a new line of merchandise as well."

"The King William? I know that place. Know of it, that is," I added hastily. "It's not far from the high street, is it?"

"On Market Street. Just the other side of the Plaza. Two minutes' walk from where Laney died. Hold on to that thought; we'll come back to it. How about coffee?"

June took hers black, no sugar, and decaf. She shook her head at my cream and three lumps. "Do you know what that will do to your arteries?" she asked.

"I usually have sweeteners," I lied. "Anyhow, I allowed you the wine."

"Wine's healthy. In moderation, of course. Never mind, it's your body. Where were we?"

"Mateo Canoso and the King William."

"Ah, yes… So, Mickey puts all this together and his eyes light up, because here's his next rung on the ladder. He rushes off to his boss, and explains how he's going to stop this new drug before it gets started. It goes all the way up to the detective superintendent, who loves the idea, and Mickey gets the green light. Of course, it's all a bit rushed, but he doesn't want anyone else to get in on the act. So he rounds up some troops, gets a warrant, and in they go. Canoso is arrested, and search teams take the King William apart."

She sat back, cradling her coffee and smiled steadily. "I was on the cordon. It was beautiful. Mickey was running in, out, and round about, all gung-ho and excited… But as the search went on, he got more and more frantic."

"I take it they didn't find anything."

"Not a thing. No factory, no Lappies, not so much as a used spliff or a smuggled duty-free. Mickey had the teams go right through the place three times, before he slipped off quietly. All very embarrassing for the lad, and just to make it worse, Mateo starts talking about wrongful arrest, not to mention charging for repairs to his shiny new pub."

"And I suppose the – what did you call him? Detective superintendent? – he would have been a bit upset?"

"Oh yes. More than a bit. And word quickly filtered down that if Mickey doesn't get this sorted out fast, then his next posting is going to be custody sergeant at the most remote station still open. Well, with that sort of threat hanging over him, Mickey got to work and did what he should have done in the first place. Ran some background checks, dug into Canoso's history. And he comes up with something useful.

"First, he finds that Canoso is a bit of a strange name. It actually means 'grey haired', and it was the name taken by Mateo's dad when he moved to Spain. From England."

"His dad's English?"

"Was. Died a few years back. And not just from England, but from this part. What's more, the old man was a bit of a lad in his day. Did some serious time – ten years for armed robbery; would have been more but they couldn't actually link him to a weapon – and then got into the drug business. Not proved, though, and when things started getting a bit hot he skipped off to Spain – where, it seems, he had a nice little family set up all ready for him. Including Mateo. Changed his name to Canoso, which might have been a sort of joke due to the fact that he apparently had long grey hair. And that his real name was Grey. Andrew Grey."

June was looking at me intently as she said this. But the significance hadn't escaped me.

"Grey?" I asked incredulously. "As in Laney Grey?"

"That's right. Andrew Grey, aka Andrew Canoso, was her father. She was Mateo's half-sister."

I sat back, struggling with the implications.

"This got Mickey all excited again," June continued, "because Laney's a well-known local figure. She's got access to all sorts of places – schools and colleges, community centres, all the venues where she did workshops and poetry readings and the like."

"All the sorts of places that were targeted by La Paz in Spain!"

"Right. And Mickey's got a whole new line of inquiry. He gets right on it, starts digging into Laney's history, and gets some

surveillance on her. He wants to know everything about her –
where she goes, who she sees, and especially if she meets with
Mateo. And they get something. CCTV picks her up crossing the
Plaza, coming from the direction of the King William. But by the
time they've phoned the CID office to let them know..."

I closed my eyes, knowing what was coming. To my surprise,
I felt a hand on mine. I opened my eyes again, and looked at her.

"It wasn't your fault, Rob. They were following her, so it was
all on CCTV. I didn't know that myself at the time, but it's clear
enough. She stepped out in front of you. You never had a chance
to miss her."

"Thanks," I muttered.

She released my hand, but not my gaze. "Don't lose sight of
that. No matter what people are saying about you."

I needed to move the conversation on. "So what did Mickey
do?"

"You know what he did. He came after you."

"Yes – but why? Like you said, it was an accident. What's he
got to gain by rattling my cage?"

She played with her spoon, twirling it round in the dregs of
her coffee. "He wasn't convinced at first that it was an accident. He
was more than half certain that it was a hit, perhaps arranged by a
rival gang." She saw my expression, and shrugged. "OK, I know it's
daft. But Mickey's getting desperate now, having lost his only lead,
and he's not the sort of man to let facts get in the way of a good
theory. And to be fair, your job would be a good cover for moving
drugs around."

"Not possible," I said firmly. "Every package we deliver has a
full audit trail, all the way from the factory till it's signed for by the
customer."

"And you check the contents yourself?"

"Well, no, but..."

"And do you ever have extra little deliveries, off your usual
routes?"

I thought of the Fiesta runs, and felt a sudden moment of doubt. Sometimes the odd package might go out without all the usual paperwork. Cutting corners to help out a customer in an emergency – that's what Colin said. Of course, he did most of the Fiesta runs himself…

Colin as a drug runner? I shook my head. "That's ridiculous!"

"Of course it is." She grinned at me. "But you can see how Mickey could start to build a case – at least in his head. And he has this thing he does, this 'investigative strategy'." She wiggled her fingers in the air to indicate the inverted commas, and expressed her opinion of it with a sneer. "He calls it 'pushing buttons and seeing what lights up'. So that's why he had a word with you. He reckoned that if you were dodgy, he only needed to push your buttons to get a result."

"Sounds a bit random to me. Does it ever work?"

"It did once. By accident. When Mickey was still a new DC, he was supposed to get a statement from the injured party in an assault. But he got the addresses mixed up, and went to see the main suspect instead. Real Keystone Kops moment, and it could have gone so badly wrong… But Mickey got lucky. When he turned up, the suspect assumed he was there to nick him, and decided to get in first with a confession. So Mickey got the arrest, and turned his cock-up into a new technique for investigation."

"Well, it didn't work with me, obviously. So why is he still on my case?"

"He was already pushing the boundaries when he came to see you. At that point, it was still an RTC and I was the officer in charge. But then the toxicology report came back on Laney. She was dosed up with La Paz."

In my mind, I saw her again. That tiny, eternal instant played out in front of me once more. But now it was different. Now I understood the terrible calmness in her face as she stepped out and looked towards me.

"You OK?"

I focused on the present, and forced a smile. "Yes. Just remembering."

"Ah. Well – now Mickey had a definite link with La Paz. Everything pointed to Laney having taken the stuff at the King William, walked over to the high street, and stepped out in front of the next large vehicle that came along. But he couldn't act on it. He'd already blown his chance. He couldn't get another warrant to search the pub – not without better intel. So he decided to keep on hassling you. Not now because he thought you did it deliberately. Even Mickey couldn't sustain that theory. But he thinks that someone must be a bit annoyed over what happened. Perhaps enough to come looking for payback. So he puts all your details out there in public and – since he can't get the funds for a proper surveillance, not now – he drops vague hints about getting into CID, and gets a dumb young copper to spend his rest day watching your flat."

"He's using me as bait!"

"Pretty much. Or pressing buttons, as he'd put it. To see if anything lights up."

"That's... bizarre."

"I'd use words like 'unprofessional', 'unethical', or 'outright illegal'. I suppose 'bizarre' fits as well. But this is Mickey Fayden we're talking about here. He's desperate, out of his depth, and he doesn't think the normal rules apply to him."

"And you're sure about this?"

"Well, most of it. I've been talking to a friend in CID – not everyone there has joined the Mickey Fan Club; not at all. She filled me in on what's been going on. I didn't know about the surveillance until you told me, but it fits." She put down her cup and glanced at her watch. "Is that the time? I'd better get going. I'm on an early tomorrow, and there's still things I need to do this evening." She stood up.

"Hey – just a minute! Is that it?"

She gave me a quizzical look. "You're all up to speed now. What else do you want?"

"Well… what can I do about it?"

"Do?" She raised an eyebrow. "Well, I suppose you could write to the chief constable and complain about your details being made public. You'd probably just get some bland standard letter that sounded vaguely apologetic without actually admitting anything, but it might put a bit of extra pressure on Mickey, which could only be a good thing."

"But what about all the newspaper stories?"

"Not much you can do about that. Don't talk to the press. That interview you gave was disastrous."

"I didn't know he'd twist everything like that."

"Reporters come in good, bad, and ugly. He's one of the ugly ones. Don't let it get to you. They'll be off your back soon."

"You can't be sure of that," I said gloomily.

"Oh, I'm pretty sure." She gave me a broad grin. "This afternoon I arrested a certain well-known sports personality for assaulting a local politician. Argument over an alleged affair with said politician's wife. It all happened in public, so no chance of keeping it covered up – it's all over the twitternet now, and it'll fill the front pages tomorrow. Don't worry, Rob; you're old news."

"Oh. Good." I felt vaguely deflated.

"As long as you don't do anything to attract attention, this should soon blow over," she continued. "Keep your head down, stay off social media, and ignore anyone who seems to be watching you. Mickey can't keep it up much longer, and he's got no more buttons to press. Thanks for the meal!"

I watched her till she had disappeared through the door, then went over to the bar and ordered a bottle of cider. Given the example June had set, I thought I could indulge myself that much at least. I sat and sipped it slowly, reflecting on the mountain of information I'd been given. Especially about Laney. I knew so much more about her now. There was still so much to learn.

After a while, I realized I was staring into an empty bottle and attracting sharp looks from the staff, wondering why I was still taking up space in their pub. Time to go home.

I had no intention of getting back into my flat the same way as I'd gone out. Apart from my personal injuries, there was the stress on Harold's marriage to consider. But neither did I want to be spotted going back in – that would make it obvious that I had sneakily managed to get out without being seen, which in turn would imply that I had something to hide. I didn't need to give Mickey Fayden any more excuse to press my buttons.

So I parked up a few streets away and approached my front door cautiously, peeping round the corner of the street before I stepped out.

The Corsa was gone. But in its place was another car that I'd never seen there before: a big, shiny, black Range Rover Evoque. Top of the range model, probably worth about fifty grand on the road, and as out of place on my street as a penguin in the desert.

I couldn't see anyone inside, but between tinted glass and poor street lighting, I wouldn't have expected to. So it might have been empty. It might have been nothing to do with me. It might have been quite safe for me to go back home.

And it might have been Elvis behind the wheel, but I didn't think that either.

What I needed was more information, and I could only think of one person to go to for that. I pulled out my phone and called June. It was reasonable to assume that she wouldn't be too pleased to hear from me again, so I jumped straight in with an apology.

"June, I'm really sorry to be bothering you again, and I know you're busy, but I seriously need your help."

"Rob?" She sounded wary, but at least not angry or even irritated. And thank goodness there were no sounds of another person in the background, which I've always found makes it a difficult conversation when you phone a girl. "What is it?"

"I've just got back. The Corsa's gone…"

"So Andy Hart got fed up and went home."

"… but there's another car there now. A black Range Rover. Do you know whose it is?"

Her voice sharpened. "What's the registration?"

"Ah. Didn't see that. Hold on a moment."

I had another quick look round the corner. "I can't make out the whole thing from here, but the last three letters are C-O-P."

"Thought so. That's Mickey Fayden's car."

"You mean he's here himself?"

"Seems so. Unless he's lent it to someone else, but that's not like him. He doesn't share his toys. Rob, I'm worried about this. If he's going to this much trouble in person, then he's taking this surveillance far more seriously than I'd realized. He may even have some sort of official backing for it."

"Some sort? What does that mean?"

"A nod and a wink from the DI, probably. No budget, no overtime, but his back's covered, and if he turns something up, it'll be feathers in caps all round."

"So how do I get home?"

"The same way that you got out, I suppose."

"No. That particular route…" I paused. That particular route was dangerous and illegal, but I couldn't say that to June. "… is no longer available," I finished. "I suppose I'll have to go to a hotel for the night."

"Yes, that's a good idea. No! Wait a minute – you paid cash for the meal, didn't you?"

"Yes. But the sweet course cleaned me out. I'll have to use my card."

"Best not to. Card transactions can be traced."

"Would he go that far?"

"It depends how much official backing he has. I don't think it's worth risking. Is there anyone else you can stop with?"

"No." I suddenly felt very lonely. "I don't have any mates that close. None that wouldn't ask awkward questions. Looks like I'll be sleeping in the car tonight." There was no immediate reply from June, so I continued. "I'll drive a bit further away and park up. I'll check again tomorrow; see if I'm still being watched. Thanks for your help, June. I do appreciate it."

"Wait a minute, Rob. Sleeping in your car isn't a good idea. For one thing, coppers notice things like that. And your face is too well known at the moment. If word gets back to Mickey…"

"OK. But what the heck am I going to do, then?"

She sighed. "Number 24 Northumberland Avenue. It's just off Eastgate Road. Do you know the area?"

"Yes, it's on one of my regular delivery routes. But…"

"Don't park outside the house. There's a public car park at the end of the street. Leave your car there. It'll be safe enough; a lot of locals use it for overnight parking."

"Yes, but whose address is it?"

"Mine, of course! Don't be too long getting here. I want to go to… I mean, I need to get some sleep."

She hung up, leaving me standing there with an entirely inappropriate smile on my face. My non-date was working out better than most of my actual dates.

Number 24 Northumberland Avenue was a neat little semi in a nice area. Young professionals on their way up, respectable retireds winding down, and unattached police officers, it seemed.

June had obviously been looking out for me, and opened the door as I approached. She'd changed into grey joggers and a plain blue T-shirt, her hair looked damp, and she had a wary expression on her face.

"Just so that we understand each other right from the start, we still didn't have a date earlier, and you are sleeping in the spare bedroom. Are we clear?"

I nodded vigorously. "Yes. Absolutely. And I'm very grateful for this, June."

"So you should be."

She led the way into the living room – actually, a combination living/dining room that ran from the front to the back of the house. TV and sofa at one end, glass-topped table at the other. It wasn't overly feminine, not many frothy frilly bits, but it was all tidy and well organized. A lot more so than my place, certainly. There was an open laptop on the table, with marked books, highlighted printouts, and an A4 pad covered in notes scattered around it.

"Sorry to interrupt your studying." I nodded at the table. "What is it – Open University?"

"Sergeant's exam. It's coming up next week, so I'm trying to get as much in my head as possible." She gave me a wry smile. "Don't worry, I hate revising, so I was glad of the excuse to leave it."

"I'm sure you'll show Mickey Fayden how it's done."

The smile disappeared, replaced by a frown. "It's got nothing to do with Fayden. I was always planning to move up. But in my own time."

"Oh. Yes, of course." I hastily took my foot out of my mouth and changed direction. "Have you had any more thoughts about why he's watching me?"

She shook her head. "It makes no sense. I can understand him getting someone like Andy Hart to hang around outside your flat – pushing buttons, like I said before – but for him to be there in person suggests he's taking the idea of you being involved way too seriously. I can't imagine that even Mickey really believes that. I'm just wondering…"

"What?"

"I'm wondering if Mickey has got some intelligence on this. Something I don't know about."

"What sort of intelligence?"

She gave me a long look. "Well… if he knows about some credible threat."

"Credible threat? You mean – a threat against me?" I thought of inflammatory newspaper articles and spray-painted words.

"Why don't you sit down?" She nodded at the sofa, and

perched on an almost matching armchair opposite. "Don't get alarmed. It's just that the newspaper article has already produced some reaction. If Mickey's got his ear to the ground, he may have heard of something else. Perhaps someone's been talking about doing more than graffiti. And catching someone making a direct assault on you would, from his point of view, be very useful. It would give him a new line of inquiry. Might even lead back to Canoso."

"He'll want revenge for his sister!" I burst out.

"Don't get carried away; it's just a theory."

It sounded all too plausible to me, and I said so. "Revenge killings are a big thing in Spain, aren't they? They're very big on family and honour and that sort of thing."

June rolled her eyes. "I think it's bigger in novels than in real life. I'm sure that this is more about what Mickey hopes will happen than anything else."

"But he must have heard something to go to all this trouble in person! You just said it yourself, June. There must be a credible threat."

"Well, if there is, you're safe enough here, aren't you? Look, you need to get some sleep, Rob. Go and have a shower if you like; I've put a clean towel out for you and there's a new toothbrush by the sink. Go and clean up – you still look like you were dragged through a hedge backwards. I'm going to have some hot chocolate – do you want one?"

It was good advice. I certainly felt better for the shower, even though I had to put the same torn and muddy clothes back on, and sipping hot chocolate afterwards made me feel more like a normal person again. June had put some music on in the background – something bluesy, not really my thing but it went well with the mood – and we talked about unimportant things. Where we came from, where we went to school, how long we'd lived here, and so on. The remarkable thing was that we had absolutely nothing in common. There were no amazing coincidences, no shared dates. It seemed that we had never been to the same places, never met the same people, never had the most remote crossing of paths.

Not until Laney.

Finally, she glanced at the clock and frowned. "Dammit, look at the time. I meant to have an early night." She stood up. "OK, I'm off to bed then. I'll be up at five tomorrow. Feel free to sleep in, and help yourself to breakfast. Not a lot in, I'm afraid, so don't expect a full English."

"That's OK. I usually manage with coffee and toast."

"Hmm. There's coffee, but it's decaf. I get enough caffeine at the station; I try and avoid it at home."

"I'm sure I'll manage. And I'll get out of your way after that."

She shook her head. "It'd probably be better for you to stay here. Keep your head down and stay out of sight. I'll ask a few questions when I get in – see if I can find out what's going on."

"Can you get the surveillance lifted?"

She shrugged. "I'll have to be careful. I'm not supposed to know about it, after all. But I'll give you a call as soon as I have something, OK? Goodnight."

"Goodnight, June. And thanks again."

She smiled. "This is going to cost you, you know. Once this is over, you're buying me dinner – and I'll want more than a Super Sharer Stag Platter!"

I smiled back. "Don't forget the large cheesecake. No problem!"

DAY 6: HISTORY

I slept in. Not surprisingly, perhaps – it had been a long and exciting day. I finally dragged myself up at about half past nine, went downstairs, and fumbled around the kitchen for breakfast.

When June had said that there wasn't a lot in, she wasn't joking. I found the decaf coffee, but no sugar to go in it, which ruled out the two main things I needed to kick-start my brain. There were some sweeteners, but they didn't really have the same effect. The only cereal was bran flakes, so my desperate search for a sugar rush eventually led me to toast and marmalade. I sat munching, and watched morning TV for a while, but found it too intellectually challenging in my decaffeinated state.

Besides, I had far too much else to think about. My head was still buzzing from everything June had told me. Strangely, though, the biggest revelation of all – that Laney had been blissed-out on La Paz when she stepped in front of me – was the easiest thing to accept. Perhaps because it took the guilt one step further away from me.

But the window that had been opened into her earlier life – that was somehow more of a shock. There wasn't a hint in any of her poems that she came from a family of criminals.

Or was there? She had had a way of laying down multiple layers of meaning in her writing – could there be something I'd missed? I needed to revisit her poems, just as soon as I could get back home.

I wandered round June's house, trying to look at things without feeling nosey. I was ridiculously pleased to find a pair of socks stuffed into some trainers and tossed in a corner. I also found that the garage, though mostly full of assorted junk, had had a small gym squeezed into it. Including a treadmill. It reminded me that I hadn't had a good workout or been for a run since the accident, and I felt the need. Of course, I didn't have any kit with me, but perhaps a short jog at least?

My thoughts were interrupted by my phone. I'd allocated a ringtone to June – not that anyone else knew the number – so I answered straight away.

"Hi, June. Did you find anything out?"

"Yes, and it's all sorted. You can go home; the surveillance has been lifted."

"That's brilliant! How did you manage it?"

"Well, actually I can't take the credit," she admitted. "Mickey screwed it up himself. Apparently he'd talked a PCSO into watching your flat from midnight on. And he'd sent Cadenti to take over from her in the morning. But she'd had a shift change and was supposed to be on an early. So she rolls in late and struggling to keep her eyes open, her sergeant has a few words, and she tells him she's been on a job for CID. Nice lass, but not the sharpest tool in the box. Of course he goes straight to the inspector about it. The inspector's not happy either, and takes it higher, and by the time Mickey wanders in for his morning coffee, it's hit the fan and is flying all over the station."

"Nice!"

"It certainly was. Mickey and his DI have been summoned to HQ to explain themselves. No doubt he'll manage to talk himself out of it, smooth git that he is, but in the meantime you're in the clear."

"Great. Well, thanks again, June. I definitely owe you that dinner."

There was a pause. "I was just joking about that, Rob. In fact, it would be best if we didn't have any contact at all after this. The force has strict rules about relationships with members of the public that we meet in the course of our duties. Unprofessional conduct. I'm already way over the line. I can't let it go any further."

"Oh. I see. Well, of course. But maybe when this is all over?"

"I don't know. Perhaps. We'll see. But not now, OK? And try not to be obvious when you leave. There shouldn't be anyone around at this time of day, but slip out the back way."

"OK."

"Bye, Rob. Take care of yourself."

She broke the connection before I could say anything else. I was disappointed that I couldn't arrange a real date with her – but she'd said "perhaps", and perhaps wasn't no.

As soon as I got home I fired up my laptop and revisited the first two books, re-reading the poems with a new point of view, trying to see anything that pointed to her father's dodgy dealings. But if it was there, it was too subtle for me to spot.

There was still her third and final collection. She'd called it *Being Seen*, and the significance of the title was clear from the first piece. It was about giving a performance; about standing up and literally being seen, being watched and judged by an audience. "I Would Like to Read for You" was insightful and honest and amusing, very Laney, and described the experience in typically fine detail. All her fear, her nervousness, the sheer riskiness of putting herself up there.

But also the drive, the desire to share what she had, the passion to let the words out and show to the world the things she saw and felt. It wasn't just her physical presence that she wanted to be seen; it was her spirit.

As I read on through the collection, I realized that it wasn't just about Laney being seen.

There were kids, playing. They were seen. Laney saw and recorded their exuberance and joy, their total absorption in their game. She also saw the bullying and selfishness, the pecking order, the little power structures they developed. Their humanness was seen.

She turned her attention to other groups as well. Shoppers, drinkers, workers, ramblers. Office staff on a lunch break, teachers in a staffroom – she saw them with a searing honesty that exposed to the world things about themselves that they probably had never been aware of. And probably wouldn't want to be.

Definitely wouldn't in some cases. She was scathing about some people. Politicians who traded principles for votes. Businessmen who put profit before people. Celebrities who were all about glamorous lifestyles but gave no thought to the effect that had on others; she spent two pages describing some starlet's hair, clothes, and make-up before finishing with a line that undermined it all:

> *And is it any wonder that our young eyes are so*
> *   dazzled by your light,*
> *That we fail to see your shadow world, which is all*
> *   of us and most of you.*

Laney had moved on in her writing, I thought. The first two books were primarily about her – her situation, her feelings. Now she was turning her gaze outwards, seeing more of the world around her. Seeing more into the world around her.

I caught myself thinking that thought and shook my head in bemusement. Laney hadn't moved on as far or as fast as I had. A week ago I had been a man who barely glanced at newspapers, and now I was reading a poem that talked about hair and clothes and jewellery. Not only reading it, but trying to understand it.

Trying? I thought I was doing a pretty good job of getting a handle on Laney's words. But how much of Laney herself was I understanding?

I wasn't sure. The person came through clearly enough – passionate, insightful, caring – but the events that made that person were much less clear. From the first book I had felt a sense of lostness, loneliness even. The second book was a return, a homecoming, a new start. In the third, someone more settled, more assured, able to look round and take stock, came across. But there was no hint of anything criminal in her past. No reference to Andrew Grey.

I decided to try another approach, and Googled his name. It didn't bring up much – not about the Andrew Grey I was interested in – but after following a lot of links, I eventually came across a newspaper article about him. From the same local paper, in fact, that had done such a comprehensive job of trashing me. So I was inclined to take their reporting with a large pinch of salt; but in fact there wasn't much to it. Just a straightforward summary of the judge's sentencing. Andrew Grey had gone down for ten years.

I dug around a bit more. The sentences all related to an armed robbery. A series of them, in fact; all with the same MO. Quiet little banks and village post offices were targeted. Just before closing time three masked men would burst in with shotguns and pistols, threatening the staff and any customers present, and make off with whatever cash was on hand. It was fast and frightening, and the gang had pulled it off at half a dozen places all round the country.

But it wasn't very lucrative, it seemed – or not sufficiently so. Having perfected their technique, the gang moved up to a city centre bank with richer pickings. And that was when things went wrong. City centre meant more people around, more staff to be threatened, and more money to collect. Which all took a little longer and attracted more attention. As the gang made their escape, a crowd gathered – then dispersed rapidly as shots were fired. Into the air, initially. But then a copper turned up. A young PC on his beat, unarmed of course. It was never entirely clear if he had challenged them or had just been trying to get people to safety. But then there was another shot. The PC took a pistol bullet in the heart and died almost at once.

The gang made their escape, but a huge police operation followed. The getaway car was found within a few hours, and witness reports indicated it had been abandoned only a short time before. Police flooded the area. Every door was knocked on, every vehicle was searched; every garage, shed, outhouse, and lock-up in a five-mile radius was opened up.

They found the money and the weapons buried on a council allotment, less than a mile from the car. The guns had been wiped clean, but a partial fingerprint was developed on a brass cartridge case in the revolver. The same weapon that had killed the PC. The fingerprint gave a name, which led to a location and a string of other suspects. They made the first arrest forty-eight hours after the robbery, and had the entire gang in custody within a week.

The cop killer got life. Twenty years apiece for the other two with guns. Andrew Grey had got off lightly, it seemed. He'd been the driver, and had never handled the guns – at least, that was his story. The prosecution alleged that he had planned everything, had obtained the guns, and recruited the others – but they hadn't been able to prove it. Even so, ten years seemed a light sentence under the circumstances. The reporter speculated that Grey had done a deal, but they had nothing to back it up with. And I wasn't inclined to give much credibility to anything I read in a newspaper.

I wondered how all this might have affected Laney. She would have been about four when her dad went off to prison. Young enough to miss him; too young to understand what was going on.

I searched for any indication of his release, but that's not the sort of thing that newspapers usually report. A man convicted of a crime is news: a hardened criminal released into the community isn't. But if he'd served his full term, Laney would have been fourteen when he got out. She'd done most of her growing up without a father.

Fourteen… that rang a bell. Something else had happened when she was fourteen.

I racked my brain, but the connection didn't come. I knew where I might find it – on Laney's website – but I was reluctant to go there. The hammering I'd got on the forum last time had been bad enough. I didn't want to think about what the Laney fans would be saying now, let alone read it.

June's warning against social media came to mind. I hadn't given it much thought at the time, since I wasn't actually on any social media. I tried it once, but there were only so many pictures of cute, fluffy animals and other people's meals I could cope with. Perhaps I had the wrong friends.

On the other hand, I didn't need to go on the forum at all, let alone actually post on it. I just needed to research her history.

I'd bookmarked the page. One click took me straight to it.

Unfortunately, I'd bookmarked the forum, and before I could stop myself I'd read the new banner that topped the page: "A MESSAGE FROM THE WEBSITE MODERATOR. PLEASE READ BEFORE POSTING ON THE FORUM." I hadn't realized that the site had a moderator. I had assumed that Laney had run it herself, and that without her it would simply remain as she'd left it. Obviously I was wrong.

The message continued in a smaller font:

As the webmaster and moderator of this forum, I consider it my responsibility to maintain it in a way that makes it a fitting tribute to Laney. I have tried to do this with a light touch, as she always valued different viewpoints and encouraged lively debate. However, a number of recent posts have gone well beyond this and have demonstrated a degree of anger and a viciousness of attitude that Laney would have found unacceptable.

I am referring in particular to some of the things that have been said since the recent newspaper article naming Robert Seaton as the van driver involved in the accident. As it happens, I have met Mr Seaton, and can assure you that he is not at all the sort of person depicted in the article. Far from being an uncaring killer, he has been deeply affected by Laney's death and has brought flowers to her memorial at North Street Library. And it should also be remembered that as far as is known at present,

Laney's tragic death was a complete accident. While this will not be officially confirmed until the inquest, there is absolutely no reason to believe that Mr Seaton was in any way to blame for what occurred.

I do understand the pain and deep sense of loss that many of you are feeling. I fully share it. But that does not justify the level of vitriol that has been directed against Mr Seaton on this site. I am quite certain that Laney herself would not have wanted this. Moreover, some posts have verged on incitement to violence, which could be a criminal offence.

I have therefore removed all those comments which I believe to be offensive, inaccurate, and demeaning to Laney's memory, and I will continue to do so. I have also written to the editor of the newspaper in question to complain about the article and to suggest that it owes Mr Seaton an apology.

Please remember that this site is about Laney and her poetry. Let's keep it appropriate to her memory, in words and in attitude.

Thank you.

I sat back. It had got difficult to read towards the end, as the words started to blur and I had to keep rubbing my eyes. It was nice to have someone on my side. Two someones, counting June. And there was Colin as well, come to think of it. A fan club of three! Not huge, but it felt vastly better than me against the rest of the world.

But who was this person? The author was shown as "BookLady", and I'd come across her before. She'd made that mysterious comment about the black gull, which I still hadn't found any reference to. However, the real clue was the mention of the library memorial. The only person who knew I'd left flowers there was the librarian who'd been on duty that day – and anyone she'd mentioned it to.

Such as her colleague, Sandra. I'd talked to Sandra about Laney. She'd known her well. And "BookLady" obviously fitted. Perhaps I should go and have another talk with her.

DAY 6: HISTORY

Wondering when the library opened, I was shocked to realize that it was half past four in the afternoon. Laney had stolen another day from me. I'd had nothing to eat since toast and bran flakes at June's, and I didn't have much in the house. I decided to skip the library and go shopping. Maybe go for a run later.

The clouds were gathering again. I felt the first few drops as I was walking home with my shopping, and got back inside just in time to avoid a soaking. No running tonight. Perhaps I should get a treadmill like June's? Not that I had space to put one. Once again, I thought about moving. The idea was becoming more and more appealing.

I stood at the window, watched the rain hammering into the rubbish-strewn back yard, and wondered how I could have lived here so long without noticing what a dump it was.

There was a feeling of change in the air. Or maybe in me. A sense that something was inexorably shifting into a new pattern. Laney's passing had begun a process that couldn't be stopped, and I was caught in the middle of it.

DAY 7 : THE BLACK GULL

I slept in late again. However, this time there was a plentiful supply of caffeine and sugar to kick-start my brain with. After a proper breakfast, I felt bold enough to check the local news and was relieved to find myself no longer part of it. As predicted, the big headlines were made by juicier stories: infamy was just as fleeting as fame itself.

Outside, the heavy clouds were finally breaking up and some sunshine was getting through. "'Forceful sunbeam, intent of purpose, muscling past the ineffectual grasp of bouncer clouds, gate-crashing through to Earth'," I said aloud, remembering something Laney had written. Then shook my head, bemused. Quoting poetry now?

Neither the Corsa nor the Range Rover was there. Of course, that didn't preclude there being another copper around somewhere, but I hoped that if the surveillance was back on, June would have let me know. Not that it mattered; I was only going to the library.

With the improving weather, I walked the mile or so, and was pleased to see that Sandra was on duty. And she was gratifyingly pleased to see me as well. As she finished stamping some books she glanced up, saw me, and gave me a wide smile.

"Mr Seaton!"

"Is it *Mrs* Deeson?"

"Yes, but I hate it. Not being Mrs; just being called it. Sandra, please. I don't do formal very well."

"OK, and I'm Rob. But are you also BookLady?"

"You've been on Laney's website? Silly question. Obviously you have. How did you know it was me?"

I explained my deductions. "I really wanted to thank you for your support. You've no idea what it meant to me."

Sandra smiled and nodded. "I understand. That article was horrendous. The reporter… well, I know his work, he's got a reputation for being able to squeeze a story out of nothing, but this time he went well over the top. And I told the editor that."

"Thanks again, but these people seem to do whatever they like, regardless."

"Don't be too sure of that. I know the editor, as it happens, and I often have letters or articles printed. They do listen if you make the right noises, and I think he understood that he needs to keep his rottweiler on a shorter leash. They should stay off your back now."

"I hope you're right."

"We'll see." she said it firmly, making the words into a promise. "And how are you doing with Laney's poems?"

"Pretty good, actually," I said with some pride. "I'm on her third book now, and I think I'm really getting a handle on them. But there was something I meant to ask you about. You put something on the forum about a black gull? Only, I can't find any reference to a black gull anywhere in her poems. So where does it come from?"

"Ah, yes." She glanced over to where Laney's memorial was still evident, though the pile of flowers seemed to have been set in better order, and older bunches removed. "Let's go and sit over there."

We settled ourselves in chairs opposite the memorial. "She used to sit just there when she was giving readings." Sandra spoke softly, staring at Laney's chair as if she could still see her in it. "When I could, I'd come and listen in. One time, she was talking to a group about symbols that poets used, and how they often might be quite unique and individual to that writer. So to really understand what the writer was saying, you had to understand their symbolism."

"The black gull is a symbol?"

She nodded and continued. "Gulls in general were special to Laney. She told us about going to the seaside and seeing the gulls for the first time. She loved the way they flew, and the way they followed fishing boats out to sea, and the way they glided low overhead when she was out on the pier. Of course (she said) she knew now that they were just looking for food, scavenging for scraps. But to a child, they were all about freedom. And that's what gulls symbolize in her writing. Freedom, life, wonder, beauty."

"I can see that. It was in that poem from her first book. The one with the injured wing, so it couldn't fly – that was about freedom being taken away!"

Sandra smiled at my excitement. "You've got it."

"But the black gull?"

"Getting to that. Laney also told us about another childhood experience. She was feeding a flock of gulls, scattering crumbs for them, when this huge black bird flapped down and started to steal the food, driving off all the gulls. It was probably a crow, or even a raven, but little Laney shouted to her mum to chase away 'the big black gull'. And after that, the 'black gull' was her symbol for evil, for bad things, for death even. She used to have nightmares about this black gull pursuing her."

"I see. That's what you meant in your post. But she never actually used it in any of her writing, did she? Or have I missed something?"

"No. It's not in any of her published work. But there's some of her writing that didn't get into the books. One piece in particular, which might have been the last thing she ever wrote…" Sandra's voice trailed off. She found a tissue somewhere, but didn't use it; just sat and stared at it.

86

"Sorry," I said round a lump in my own throat.

"It's all right. It's just that…" She put the tissue to use, wiping her eyes, before continuing. "Laney used to send me bits of her work all the time. She liked me to read them over, give her feedback. I helped her put things together for publication, researched possible markets, set up the website. It was one of the best times of my life, seeing this wonderful talent blossoming and maturing – and being able to be part of it. Hours we spent together, talking poetry. Then, when I heard about the accident…"

She went silent again. I joined in.

"My turn to say sorry." She glanced at me. "This must bring it back for you."

"It does," I admitted. "But I need to go there. I can't deal with it by hiding from it. And I need to get to know her. To understand who she was and what she was like, so that it might make some sort of sense. Because if she was just a… a random person, just a figure I knocked down, then it doesn't mean anything. But she wasn't; she was real and unique and special, and I have to get hold of that to give it some sort of value." I stopped, bemused by what had just tumbled out of my mouth. "That doesn't make sense, does it?"

Sandra gave me a gentle smile. "Actually, it does. So then, I was saying… The day after the accident, an envelope arrived here for me. Laney's handwriting. But I didn't open it. I couldn't. Not for several days. Because I knew it was the last one I'd ever get from her, and when I opened it she really would be gone. And that doesn't make any sense at all!"

"Of course it does."

"I only opened it yesterday, and it was a new poem. About a black gull."

She got up and went over to a filing cabinet behind the reception desk. After a brief rummage she was back with a large brown envelope.

"What do you make of this?" She handed it to me, but then

headed back to deal with another customer, leaving me alone with Laney's last words.

The envelope had been neatly slit open. I reached in and hesitantly withdrew the single sheet of lined paper inside.

I hadn't seen Laney's handwriting before. She wrote large. Clear, bold italics that filled the paper. There was no title; she just launched into it.

> *Whilst grey gulls soar free above salt water,*
> *And send their cry across the shifting valleys,*
> *The Black Gull makes its nest in darker places,*
> *Deep in the grave of a forgotten past,*
> *Once resplendent for all to see,*
> *Now cast down, its glory tarnished.*
>
> *There it lays its doom-full eggs,*
> *And hatches its poisonous brood,*
> *Of unnatural heaven,*
> *And guards it well,*
> *Secure behind an armoured web.*
> *Which does not,*
> *yield,*
> *Save to the knowing hand,*
> *That which is empty.*
>
> *I will not share its bitterness*
> *I will not live in its shadow*
> *I will take its gift and find a cleaner peace.*

"What do you think?" Sandra had come back and was reading over my shoulder.

"It's a suicide note," I said without thinking.

Sandra gasped. "You think she killed herself?"

I mentally took myself outside, gave myself a good kicking, and reminded myself that most of the things June had told me were not yet public knowledge. Such as the fact that she'd committed suicide while high on La Paz. Looking, perhaps, for a cleaner peace – but I couldn't tell Sandra that.

Instead, I shook my head vigorously. "No, it's just this bit about finding peace. That's the first thing that came to mind. But you know how Laney always had several layers of meaning. What was she actually saying here?"

"That's just it. I'm really not sure. It's somehow different from her other writing. There's things in it that I just don't get at all. These odd lines in the middle, for one thing: 'Which does not/ yield'. Why does she break it up like that?"

"I haven't a clue," I said, this time in complete honesty. Nothing June had told me shed any light there. "How does the black gull thing fit in, do you think?"

"Well – as I said – for Laney it was a symbol of the dark side of life. So perhaps that fits with seeking peace. You know, I wonder if you might be right about it being a suicide note. Because she was going through a difficult time. The last few weeks – she wasn't herself. She was so withdrawn. Well, she'd always had this way of retreating inside herself while she thought about something. You could tell when she'd slipped into deep-thought mode. But this was different. It was more worried. Fearful, even. And she'd lost all her brightness and humour. It was like a shadow was on her."

"Or a black gull." I patted Sandra's arm, awkwardly. "Didn't she say anything about what was troubling her?"

"No. She shut me out. In fact, I hadn't even seen her for over a week when… when it happened." She picked up the poem. "Then this. Laney's last work. And it feels so sad. Yes, perhaps it is a suicide note. But why?" She choked back a sob, and we sat silently for a moment.

I glanced at the envelope. Same handwriting, of course, but different pen. Black ink instead of blue. Thick brown paper, oversized for the single sheet of paper it had contained. I picked it up, looked at the postmark.

"Sandra," I asked slowly, "do you know if there's a post office in the Plaza?"

She nodded. "About halfway down." Her eyes widened as she made the connection. "That's just near where it happened!"

"Yes. And look at the date it was stamped. The same day!"

"She wrote this in her notebook." Sandra's voice had sunk to a whisper. "She always carried one with her. And a pen. Always jotting things down as they came to her. But then she ripped out the page, went into the post office, and sent it to me. And after that…"

"Yes. I know."

"I never even thought of looking at the postmark."

"Why would you? Who ever bothers to do that?"

"I suppose. Rob – do you think I should tell the police?"

I shrugged. "I expect so. I doubt if it'll tell them anything they don't already know, but it might help them dot some 'i's." *And it might get Mickey Fayden off my back for a while*, I added mentally. "Could I get a copy of the poem?"

"Take that one if you like. I've made copies."

"Really? But… it's the original. The last one she actually wrote."

Sandra smiled, and touched my arm. "Yes, I know. And because you know that, it feels right that you should have it. I think she'd like that as well."

She went back to work, and I sat puzzling over the poem for another ten minutes. The references to La Paz were clear enough, but most of it was still obscure.

And the timing of it had to be significant. Posting it to Sandra must have been almost the last thing Laney ever did. Which meant that it was important. Stuffed full of chemical peace, she was thinking calmly, unemotionally. Planning every action. The poem was a suicide note, as I'd first said, but I was more and more certain that there was more to it than that. I even had the glimmering of an idea about what it might be.

But I needed more information to be sure. And I could think

of only one place where I might find it. I folded the poem away in a pocket and headed for the door.

"Let me know if you have any ideas about it," Sandra called as I passed her.

"I will. Ah – if you do tell the police, you don't have to mention that I've got a copy, OK?"

She raised an eyebrow.

"I'm not asking you to lie if they ask you," I assured her. "It's just that I've had far too much connection with this already. I'd rather they didn't have another little snippet to perhaps leak to the press."

"I can understand that. I'll keep you out of it."

"Thanks." I turned to go, then another thought struck me. "Oh, Sandra – I meant to check up on something before I got sidetracked by your post. What happened when Laney was fourteen?"

She smiled. "That was her big year. The first great success she had. That was when she won the National Schools Poetry Competition." Her smile turned to a frown. "That was the good thing that happened. The bad thing…"

"I know. Her father came home."

There was only one Willdyne Street in England, according to all the search engines I'd tried, and it was ten minutes' walk from the library. A quiet suburban backwater no different from hundreds of others – except that Laney Grey had once called it home.

It hadn't changed much from the description in her poem. The street name had been relocated and was now twenty feet up on the wall. It hadn't kept it from being defaced in just the same way as its predecessors. The "d", the "n", and the "e" had been spray-painted out, no doubt to the vast amusement of the kids who did it. Old jokes don't die; they are just disinterred and resurrected by each new generation.

The corner shop had reopened as a mini-market. But the rest of the street seemed unchanged. Even number 15 still had its blue door and brass knocker, with a doorbell to the side.

I used the knocker.

There was a long pause, during which I debated knocking again or hurrying away. Before I came to a decision, a lock clicked and the door opened a short distance. There was a chain on it, I saw, and not far above the chain a clear brown eye.

"Is that the police again?" An old lady's voice, warm with Caribbean tones but shaded with apprehension.

"No, I'm not the police." It must have been a copper who had told her about Laney. Perhaps she feared that there was more bad news; I hastened to reassure her. "I only want to talk with you for a minute. You won't know me, but my name's Robert Seaton."

There was a pause while the eye looked me up and down. "I do know you, boy." The door closed, the chain rattled off, and it opened again, but wider.

She was a small woman, not much over five feet high and fine boned with it. Or you might say skinny, if you were being blunt. Neat dark clothing, dark wrinkled skin beneath crinkled grey hair, and a gentle smile that I couldn't understand if she was a relative of Laney's and if she did know who I was. I felt it had to be spelled out, in case some misunderstanding now made things worse later on. "I'm the person who was driving the van that –"

She stopped me with a raised hand. "The van that killed Laney. Yes, I know. I'm Roshawn Skerrit. Her grandmother. You'd better come in, Mr Seaton."

She led the way into the room next to the front door. It was as small and neat as she was herself, though with a slightly formal feel to it. As with many people in this part of town, she probably did most of her living in the kitchen and dining room at the back of the house, reserving the "living" room for special guests and formal occasions.

Paradoxically, this made me feel more at ease, since I'd been raised in a similar tradition. I wasn't surprised when she announced that she was going to make some tea, without asking if I would like any. It was part of the ritual, a recognized way of dealing with

92

awkward situations that gave us all some common ground, no matter what our background or experience of life was.

While water boiled and spoons tinkled on china in the back of the house, I looked round the room, and especially at the photographs, which covered the walls and stood on shelves and the mantelpiece. Many were of Laney. Some were quite recent, colour pictures of her holding up her books (I recognized the covers), talking to groups of people, shaking hands, or hugging friends. I recognized Sandra in one shot, which looked to have been taken in the library.

Others were of a much younger Laney, sometimes in school uniform, and often with a strikingly attractive woman whom I supposed to be her mother. Finally, I discovered a family group: Laney, in school uniform, holding a plaque, flanked by her (supposed) mother and a much younger-looking Roshawn Skerrit.

"That was a special time for us." She had come into the room very quietly, in spite of the tray she was carrying. I had been peering closely at the photo, trying to read the inscription on the plaque. Putting the tray down on a coffee table, she came to stand next to me.

"Was that when she won the competition?"

"That's right. A proud day for us all. We all knew that Laney had a great gift, but that was when the world knew it as well."

"Then that's her mother with you?"

"Yes, that's my girl, Elizabeth."

In my quick scan of all the photographs, I'd seen very few men. One old black and white was probably of Laney's grandma and grandad on their wedding day, but there was no similar picture of Elizabeth Grey, née Skerrit, and Andrew Grey.

"Laney's father isn't here, is he?"

Roshawn Skerrit turned away abruptly. "You'll find no picture of that man in this household." Surprisingly, there was no anger or bitterness in her voice. Just sorrow and regret. "Sit yourself, Mr Seaton. Will you take milk and sugar in your tea?"

"Yes please."

We sat in silence as she poured then handed me a cup. She sipped at her own, then offered me a plate of biscuits.

"I'm glad you came, Mr Seaton," she said abruptly.

"I wasn't sure if I should. I was afraid that I might be, well, would likely be unwelcome. Under the circumstances."

She shook her head vigorously. "I understand the circumstances. The police explained things quite well, and I know that you weren't to blame. It was a terrible thing that happened, for you as much as for anyone."

Her insight and empathy caught me by surprise. "Not everyone gets that," I muttered.

"Well, I'm an old woman, and if there's one thing I've learned in all my years, it's that tragedies aren't ours alone. There are always others caught up in these things, and their pain is just as real."

I thought of the shockwave that had expanded outwards from the moment of Laney's death, of all the people who had been touched by the hurt of it, and nodded slowly.

"Clinging to our own pain helps no one," Roshawn continued. "Keeping others in mind helps put it in perspective, at least. So I was praying for you, soon as I knew what had occurred, and then when that awful newspaper report came out, I thought how you must feel."

"Pretty bad," I admitted.

"Well, I supposed so. I wanted to speak to you then and tell you I laid no blame on you, but I then thought that it might make things worse if I did. But I have prayed that I would get a chance to speak to you, and it seems like the good Lord heard my prayer, for here you are."

I was surprised to find my eyes were stinging. "Thank you for that," I mumbled past the lump in my throat. "That's – it means a lot. Coming from you."

She nodded, and passed me a box of tissues. "No shame in tears," she admonished gently when I hesitated.

I let it all out. Being so emotional in front of a stranger wasn't something I could have imagined happening before. But just then it was the most natural thing in the world.

"There's healing in tears," she said as I came to the end of it, and indeed I felt as if a burden had been eased, if not entirely lifted. "Do you want another cup of tea? That one may be getting cool by now."

It was, but I drank it anyway. "I'm OK, thanks."

"Well then, Mr Seaton, why don't you tell me why you came?"

"I've been trying to find out more about Laney. I wanted to know who she was. I've read her poems, the published ones. And looked on her website. But there's still so much I haven't really understood – can't understand – without knowing more of her life. And who she was. So I came here, because this was where she came, in her poem, when she came home."

Roshawn nodded. Her eyes had drifted away from me, staring over my shoulder and back in time. "Oh, but that was a wonderful day! When I opened the door and saw her standing there – it was the first time I had laid my eyes on her for five years."

"Five years? Where had she been?"

"Here and there. Travelling, always moving. Hiding."

"Hiding?"

"From her father."

And suddenly, it came into focus. That was what her first book had been about. All that loneliness, that lack of involvement, the standing outside of life, looking in – it was being on the run, always hiding, never at home.

"*Postcards to Myself*!" I said.

Roshawn smiled. "Yes. While she was away, she would send me postcards. That was all the contact we had in those years, but it let me know that she was OK. I kept them, of course, and showed them to her when she came home. When she decided to publish the poems she had written during that time, she thought of the postcards, and that gave her the title."

"But why did she do that? Hide, I mean."

"Well…" She shook her head. "Where should I start?"

"Where does it begin?"

She put down her cup, stood up, and began to walk round the room, looking at the photographs.

"You've asked the right question, Mr Seaton." Pausing by her wedding picture, she stared at it for a moment, then shook her head. "No, it was after he'd gone. He was a good man, and if he'd been here it would have been different. But he died too young, too soon." She touched the frame gently, then opened the drawer beneath it and took out a small object, which she brought over to show me.

"A wedding ring?"

"Elizabeth's." A plain gold band, unremarkable to the eye, full of meaning to her. "Things hadn't been easy for her, with her father gone. We got by, but we didn't have a lot. No jewellery, no smart clothes, not many friends. She was beautiful – you can see how beautiful! – but she was always a little shy, a little awkward with people. When she met Andrew Grey… he was like something from another world. Good-looking, confident – and charming as well. Funny. He could always make her laugh. She was just nineteen; he was ten years older and once he set himself to it, she had no chance at all. Of course, we didn't know what he really was."

"A criminal, you mean?"

"A criminal, a philanderer. A trophy collector. We learned all about them, in time: the blonde woman up in Newcastle, the Chinese girl in London. One in Ireland, another in Wales – a whole family in Spain… Elizabeth was his token black girl. But we didn't realize that until too late. She was so in love with him, but she wouldn't be with him unwed. So they married, and for a while everything seemed good. Of course, he was away a lot on his 'business trips', and that was lonely for her, but she accepted that, looked forward to him coming back. Then she got pregnant."

"He wasn't happy?"

"Irritated. It was an inconvenience. He wanted her to have the baby aborted, but she refused. It was the first time she had argued with him about anything, and she saw the darkness in him then. He was violent, slapped her, then threw her out of the house... they lived some miles from here. It was a wet night, cold. She was knocking on my door at midnight, bruised and cold and soaked to her very bones. But the worst injury was the one to her soul."

We sat in silence for a while before she resumed the story.

"He came round the next morning. He had a suitcase with some of her things, and he said he was going away and she was to stay with me. And he told me not to make trouble; that he had friends in the police, and if I stirred things up he'd know about it.

"We didn't see him again until after Laney was born. Then he turned up one day, no warning, all smiles and jokes, kisses and cuddles, playing the proud father for all he was worth. Of course, we didn't believe it, but she went back with him anyway. She didn't have a choice.

"It was like that for the next few years. He came and went as he pleased; she lived in fear of him. He didn't bother to hide his violent side, and she didn't dare to cross him. Sometimes he made a fuss of Laney, mostly he ignored her. One time he threatened her, and that was more than Elizabeth could take. Next time he left the house, she packed a bag and ran. Her and her little girl. Laney was just four years of age then."

"What was she like as a child?"

Roshawn smiled at that memory. "Such a serious little thing. Oh, she laughed and played and cried and was fussy about her food, just like other children. But sometimes she would sit and stare at things, just watching for as long as we'd let her. Sunshine in the leaves, raindrops on the window, ants going in and out of a crack in the path. And when she learned to talk, the questions never stopped!"

She stood up again, went over to the mantelpiece, and picked up a framed photo. "This was her that time they ran away from him."

A slender little girl in a bright red anorak, glancing up at the camera, face full of wonder. She had an ice-cream cone in her hand, but the ice-cream was all gone, apart from a smear round her mouth. But she wasn't eating the cone. The photographer had caught her in the act of scattering pieces of it in front of her, and the view was wide enough to show the gulls gathering to squabble over the crumbs. In the background, past some railings, was a stretch of beach and the sea.

"She loved the seaside," Roshawn said. "And especially the seagulls."

I nodded. "I saw that from her poems. And I heard the story about the crow as well, that she called the Black Gull."

A look of pain crossed Roshawn's face at that. She took the photo and put it back in its place.

"That's not the full story. When Andrew Grey found them again – it didn't take him long, just a few weeks – when he came and forced them to go back with him – after that, Laney started calling him the Black Gull. Or maybe Elizabeth started it first. I don't know. I didn't get to see them for months. He kept them prisoners in their own home. They weren't allowed out of the door, not even into the garden. I didn't even know they were there for a long time. When I did find out, he wouldn't let me in the house. I sometimes stood and waited nearby for hours, just to manage a few minutes' conversation through the window while he was busy elsewhere."

I shook my head. "How could that happen? You'd think someone would notice something."

She shrugged. "If they did, they didn't say anything. Perhaps, like me, they were afraid of the consequences for Elizabeth and Laney if they spoke out. Or if they did, nothing came of it. He had friends in the police, remember."

"Not good enough to get him off an armed robbery charge! Wasn't that the same year?"

"Yes it was, and how glad I was to see some justice done at

last. Though even then he should have got longer. But at least he served his full time. There were a good many people who believed he was the one responsible for that poor young policeman getting shot, one way or another, and they made very sure that he didn't get off too lightly."

She walked round the room again, and I got up and followed her, looking at the photos she indicated. Images of Laney growing up. In school uniform. Curled up with a book. Blowing out candles on a birthday cake – a whole montage of these, from five candles all the way to fourteen. Unwrapping Christmas presents, waving from a fairground ride, digging on a beach.

"Those were the good years. The best years," she said. Not to me.

She finished by the picture I'd looked at first: three generations together, Laney with her plaque.

"We knew she was good with words. We didn't realize how good, till then. Two weeks after that, he was released."

"And he came straight back?"

"Not immediately. We hoped he'd stay away; that after ten years he'd forgotten us." A weariness seemed to touch her at that point, her posture changing as though a heaviness had come on her. She went back to her chair. "Andrew Grey was not a man for forgetting. Or forgiving, either. And the fact that Elizabeth had defied him, had tried to escape – I think that was an insult. Perhaps a threat? I don't know. How can you understand a man like him? He was a different sort of being..." Her voice trailed off.

"You don't have to say any more."

She looked at me and sat upright. "It's good that someone else should know the story, and you have more cause than most, Mr Seaton. You are part of that story now."

I nodded, and she continued.

"Andrew Grey had not wasted his time in prison. He had been preparing to go into a new line of business. Armed robbery had proven to be too risky; drugs were safer and more lucrative. When he returned here, he had already obtained his first supply, and he used it at once. On Elizabeth. He made her an addict."

"His own wife?"

"It was a means of controlling her. She was dependent on him after that. And there was always the threat he held over her: that he would do the same to Laney if she ever crossed him again." Her voice remained calm, but her eyes glistened. "I saw very little of my daughter after that. He moved them several times. His new business was successful; he had a new house every year, always bigger and more luxurious. I was not welcome in any of them, and Elizabeth was rarely allowed out. As the drugs worked their evil in her, she lost her desire to leave. He had beaten her. Laney was given some freedom; she still went to school and we met whenever we could. But that was all the social life she had. He didn't want her having any contacts outside the family. No friends – definitely no boyfriends! He had men watching her all the time. She would be taken to school, picked up from school, taken shopping. Once she was seen talking to a boy outside the school gates. He told her that if she spoke to that boy again, he would have his legs broken."

"And she stopped writing poetry."

"He'd heard about her award. He didn't like her getting public attention, and he told her to stop wasting time on 'silly scribblings'. He threw the plaque out, and told her to forget it and move on. As soon as she was old enough, he made her leave school. She had wanted to go on to university – her teachers wanted her to as well – but he wouldn't consider it. And of course, Laney couldn't defy him. She knew that her mother would suffer for it if she did."

"I can't imagine what it must have been like to live like that."

"No, you can't. No one can. No one would want to. But they did live like that. We did – for years – while my Elizabeth died slowly, a little bit each day.

"He used Laney as a housekeeper after she left school. Cooking, cleaning, looking after her mother. By then, Elizabeth was no longer capable of doing anything for herself. One small mercy: at least he never molested Laney. Even he wasn't that depraved. But he often brought women back to the house, and she had to be pleasant to them and wait on them like a servant, and keep her mother quiet.

"After a while, he began to involve her in his business. He had her run errands. Deliver packages, take messages. He let her take driving lessons because 'a pretty girl doesn't arouse suspicion'. It gave her more freedom, but she hated being part of it. She said she was giving people the Black Gull's poisonous eggs."

I nodded, thinking of her last poem.

"Elizabeth began to get worse. He controlled her supply of heroin, kept her from overdosing, but her body was losing the fight. And of course, he wouldn't let her go to a doctor. Then, one day, Laney found her dead. She had managed to keep back enough of the drug to overdose. It was her last chance to defy him and be free. She left a note. Just two words: 'Run Laney'. And she did. Grabbed a bag and left the house that same hour. Took a car, drove into town, and left it. Caught the next train out. By the time Andrew Grey found out, she'd disappeared."

"She never stopped running, did she?"

"Not for many years. And he never stopped looking for her. He had no grief for Elizabeth, but he was furious that she had killed herself, and even more that Laney had run from him. He came here, making threats, demanding to know where she was, but of course, I didn't know. Laney hadn't told me anything. And with both of them gone, there was little he could threaten me with."

"He might have attacked you. Killed you, even."

"Perhaps. But I wasn't as isolated as he had made Elizabeth and Laney. I had friends, and if something had happened to me, there would have been questions asked. And besides, he knew I was his best chance of tracing Laney. He thought she would be in touch eventually. He used to come round, unannounced, to search my mail. I think he even tapped my phone for a while. But she never called me. I didn't know where she was, or what she was doing, in all those years."

"There were the postcards."

"Never in her own name. Never saying anything about herself. She even changed her handwriting – wrote with her left hand or something. Of course, he was suspicious. He probably went to the places they were posted from. But she was never there. All the same, when I got a card I knew that she was still out there, still safe and free."

"Still running."

"Yes. Always running. Never settling."

I thought of the poems she'd written in those years, and now I understood at last where they had come from. But I also understood her later work. What it had meant when she could finally stop running and come home. I said as much to Roshawn, and she smiled. "You understand so well," she said.

"How did it happen – that she came home?"

"About five years after Elizabeth died, Andrew Grey left England for good. I heard that the police had been passed information about him and were closing in. And there were rumours about rival gangs, but I don't really know. By that time he had stopped bothering me. He'd given up on Laney making contact, and he no longer came to see if she had been here or to search my mail. He went to Spain, to his other family. And the police were right behind him, with a warrant for his arrest, so he couldn't come back. Even so, I waited a few months to be certain. Then I sent Laney a message."

She laughed when she saw my frown. "I know I said I had no contact with her. But I had had all those years to think of how it might be done. And in the end, it was simple enough. I searched for poetry sites online – oh yes, I'm quite an accomplished 'Silver Surfer!' – and began leaving messages. Well, one message, in fact: 'The Black Gull has flown.' Perhaps more cryptic than necessary – I doubt if he would ever have looked at those sites, even if he was still searching for her – but old habits die hard, as they say."

"It worked, though."

"Yes, indeed. Laney phoned me. And hearing her voice again…

It was so wonderful, neither of us could speak properly between laughter and tears. A week later she was walking through my door."

"Home again!"

"Yes. You see that picture on the wall behind me?"

"Of course." It was impossible to miss, being the largest in the room, and not a photograph but a painting. Laney, Elizabeth, and Roshawn, sitting together with hands clasped. I'd assumed that it had been done before Elizabeth's death, but looking at it now I realized that Laney was a little older than she would have been, and Roshawn a little greyer. The background, I realized, was this very room.

"Laney had that painted last year. The three of us at home together. The way it could have been."

"The way it should have been."

"Yes. But we don't get to write our own stories, do we? There was a time when I hoped that we might. I thought that at least Laney would be able to write her own life story. But it didn't happen. Instead, we had a visitor. Just a few weeks ago. A handsome young man, and very like his father. When I saw him, I thought for a moment that it was Andrew Grey again, even though we'd heard that he died."

"It must have been a terrible shock."

"It nearly stopped my heart, seeing him like that. He told us he was Laney's half-brother. Mateo Canoso, he called himself. Apparently, Grey had changed his name. He had his father's charm as well, all full of how sorry he was about the past, and how his father had died in regret over Elizabeth, and how he wanted to heal the estrangement in our family. He was very plausible. I might even have believed him, if I hadn't remembered how plausible Andrew Grey could be.

"Laney wasn't taken in either. She'd known her father even better than I had. She asked him straight out what he wanted. That put him off. I don't think he was used to people seeing through him so easily. But he told us that he'd moved to England, had started a business, and wanted Laney's help with it. He knew all about her readings and workshops, and he wanted her to put him in touch with people and to help distribute his 'merchandise'."

"Merchandise? Did he say what merchandise?" I asked, knowing full well that he'd meant La Paz.

"No, he never spelled it out. But of course we knew it would be drugs of some sort. And Laney would have nothing to do with it. She told him that. Told him that their father was a criminal; that she blamed him for her mother's death, and she wanted nothing to do with him, his family, or his business.

"He started to get angry then and the charm vanished. He told her that they were family whether she liked it or not; that he was her elder brother and that he would have proper respect from her and for their father's memory. Her mother's weaknesses were not their father's fault. He'd done everything he possibly could for her, and her ingratitude had broken his heart. So here he was now, prepared to put the past behind them and offer her a chance to make some real money, much more than she'd ever get from her scribblings."

"I don't imagine that went down well."

"No. They were standing and shouting at each other by then, him half in Spanish, and I was afraid he would hit her. And she would certainly have hit him if it had continued. I pushed my way between them, waving the telephone, and told him I'd called the police. I wish now that I had. But that got through to him. He didn't say another word; just turned and stalked out."

"But he came back."

"Not here. I never saw him again. Laney, though… I knew he must have been in touch with her. She wouldn't speak of it; she didn't want me involved. But I saw that she was carrying a burden. And of course, I knew what Canoso would be saying to her; how he would try to break her. He would be threatening to harm me. Just as his father had used Laney to control Elizabeth, and Elizabeth to control Laney. I told her to ignore that; said she should run and hide, like she had before – he wouldn't harm me if she was gone."

"She wouldn't go, would she?" I knew it as clearly as if she had been in the room telling me herself. I had read the postcards to herself. I'd understood what they really meant. I knew her now, and knew she would never have gone back to that life.

The tears were running down Roshawn's cheeks now. Tears of grief, but also of pride. "No. She would not. She told me that she would not run any more. She would face it and finish it. And then she left. I did not see her again. And when the police came to my door, I knew why. It wasn't a surprise."

We were both quiet then. For a long time.

"I don't know how…" When I finally spoke, I found I couldn't finish the sentence. But she understood.

"I take each day as it comes. Every day I think of them. Every day I grieve. And every day I remember the good times as well, and thank the Lord for them. That's important. Those things happened as well – the good times were just as real as the bad ones. And they can't take those away from me."

I stood up. "Mrs Skerrit. Thank you for sharing all this with me. I know it must be hard."

She shook her head as she stood. "It's hard, but it's also good. With all the pain, it's still good to talk to someone about them. Especially someone who understands as you do, Mr Seaton. I'm just sorry that our family tragedy has involved you."

I struggled to find something to say. "I'm sorry too. I mean, that it happened. All of this." I waved my hand, indicating the pictures, meaning the story behind them. It didn't seem the right response, but I didn't know what was.

She smiled, understanding. "What are you going to do now?"

"I think I'll go back to where it happened. I'm not sure why, but I think there's still something to learn."

"I see. You are welcome here at any time, Mr Seaton. Come again, and we will talk some more. There's still a lot I'd like to tell you about Laney."

When I got back to the flat, I changed into my running kit and went for a long jog. I took my usual route: along the backstreets, through the recreation ground, and down the canal towpath. It curves around the edge of town and brings me back to within half a mile of home – a nice circular route that usually takes me an hour at a steady pace.

Every step of the way I was thinking about the things Roshawn Skerrit had told me. The huge tragedy that had invaded her life and taken her daughter; given her a granddaughter and then taken her away as well. The amazing strength and courage that she carried in her little old lady's body.

It put my life in perspective.

DAY 8: THE BEGINNING

Next morning a package arrived for me. I'd paid top price for a quick delivery of Laney's books, but had sceptically assumed that meant at least a week, despite the promises. I mentally apologized, opened the package, and spread the contents out on the table next to my toast and marmalade.

They were thin little volumes, but somehow seemed more substantial than the digital versions on my laptop. The covers were a surprise, bright and cheerful, which seemed a strange contrast to the content that I already knew about. *Postcards to Myself* had, unsurprisingly, a picture of postcards pinned on a board below the title, all standard beach or town scenes. No waves were prominent, which to me seemed to miss an opportunity. *Stepping out of Shadow* had a picture of autumn leaves blowing in the wind, which tied in with the first poem, if not so much with the collection as a whole. The third book, *Being Seen*, had an actual picture of Laney on the cover. It was a three-quarters front view of her standing, apparently on a stage, with a book in her hand. Presumably reading to an audience.

"You got it wrong," I said to the unknown person who had designed the cover. "It's not about her being seen; it's about us being seen by her."

I had come a long way in my quest to understand Laney Grey. I'd read her words, traced her roots, and followed her path. Only one thing remained to do. I had to go back to where it had begun for me and ended for her.

I stood by a tree and watched the traffic hurtling by. It was supposed to be a forty-mile-an-hour limit, but a lot were doing well over that.

I'd been doing forty. Keeping to the limit. Hadn't I? I was sure I had. The police had confirmed it.

Just in front of me was a parked car. There was roadside parking all along this stretch, which was ridiculous on such a busy road, but there had never been adequate parking for shoppers. So they had roadside parking: thirty minutes maximum and no return for an hour. Cars were always pulling out into traffic or slowing to find a parking space. It was amazing that there weren't more accidents.

I'd forgotten about the trees. When they built the Plaza, they'd put in trees and bushes and flower beds to break up the monotony of concrete, but the trees had gone in too close to the road. They overhung the parked cars, dumping leaves and sap, and making a confusing pattern of light and shade. I had had no chance of seeing Laney until she'd stepped clear of the shadows and out into the road. By then, it was far too late.

I looked back towards the Plaza. It was Laney who'd called it "the monotony of concrete". I couldn't remember where, exactly, but it was in the third book. And now I thought about it, it wasn't *the* monotony, but *a* monotony. The collective noun for concrete.

She must have been standing just here by the tree, about where I was. The spot was marked with a pile of dead flowers in dirty plastic. The blood on the road had been cleaned up, but the tattered bouquets and handwritten messages had been left.

She'd stood and watched the traffic going past and waited for the right one. Waited for my van. She'd chosen my van because she was thinking clearly and logically. She wanted to die as quickly as possible, not lingering in agony. And with no possibility of surviving.

So she waited until she saw a big vehicle coming, something

with a lot of weight behind it. Something moving too fast to stop, right up to the speed limit. She would have seen me coming in plenty of time.

I turned away. My eyes were stinging. I wasn't over this yet. I wanted to go home.

Instead, I started walking into the Plaza, away from the road.

They'd done their best to break the monotony, or at least to disguise it. Patterns in blue and red tiles decorated the paving, trees and planters and benches punctuated the space, shops lined it. Laney would have come from that direction. Walking towards me, towards the road. Coming from… in the distance I could see the post office sign.

I walked towards it, weaving my way through the shoppers. Teenage girls giggling over their smartphones, old men overdressed for the warmth of the day. Women struggling with too much shopping, groups of kids who should have been in school. Smart business people hurrying purposefully, scruffy lads sauntering aimlessly. I pictured Laney walking towards me, in the crowd, apart from them, determined on her death and poisoned with artificial peace.

Reaching the post office I stood in the doorway, looking in. A display of envelopes was on one wall, to the right of the door. The closest ones were the largest size: brown paper, within easy reach of someone walking in, needing an envelope but not caring what sort.

So she'd walked in, picked up an envelope, gone over to the counter. There was a short queue there now. Perhaps she'd had to wait. She wasn't in a hurry. She'd taken the page torn out of her notebook, slipped it into the envelope, and sealed it; written the address on the front, using the pen chained to the counter – that was why the ink was different! And then she'd paid for envelope and postage together before leaving. On her way to meet me.

"Are you going in or what?"

I stepped aside, muttering apologies, and a harried-looking woman pushed past, glaring.

She could use some Lappies, I thought.

I carried on down the Plaza. Market Street was just a hundred yards or so from the post office. But it wouldn't have suited Laney's purpose. Too narrow, too quiet, traffic too slow. Plenty of shops along here as well, but smaller and shabbier: second-hand bookshops, greasy spoon cafés, fundraisers for obscure charities.

And the King William. A right turn out of the Plaza and a short walk round a bend in the road, and there it was: on the opposite side, at the corner of a narrow alley.

I had a vague memory of a traditional city pub, walled in green tiles. Narrow windows, shabby dark paintwork, and a disreputable air to it. The sort of place you'd go to make furtive deals with shifty characters.

It had changed considerably. For one thing, it was now the *Prince* William. There was no sign; the name was displayed on massive plate glass windows that ran the full length of the building and the full height of the ground floor. The few bits that weren't glass were shiny chrome or pale brick. The whole effect was to shout "I'm new! I've changed!" so loudly that it sounded desperate. (And when the heck had I started having thoughts like that? Just since Laney? Or had they always been there without me noticing?)

I was feeling strange. Shaky. It was as though I was coming to the end of a journey, and something was waiting for me there.

No, not the end of a journey. The beginning of one. This was where Laney had started from on the last journey of her life. I saw her stepping out of the corner set door, crossing the road – carefully, it wasn't quite her time yet – and walking towards the Plaza.

As she passed me, a question suddenly burst out: *Why, Laney?*

She didn't answer. Just met my gaze for one brief second, and then she was gone.

"You all right, mate?"

I wasn't. I was trembling violently, and my vision was so blurred that I couldn't make out the face of the concerned stranger.

"Yes. I'm fine. Just a bit of a chill. I'm fine, thanks." I wiped my eyes on my sleeve, and forced a smile.

"Well, you look like you need to go and sit down for a bit."

"You're right. I will. Thanks."

He nodded, and carried on.

It seemed like the most natural thing in the world to go into the Prince William. After all, it was two o'clock, and I hadn't eaten since breakfast. A late breakfast, but I was certainly ready for a bite now, and a pub lunch would hit the spot nicely. Plus, I did need to go and sit down.

And to reach the end of my journey, I had to see the beginning of hers.

The inside was as aggressively new as the outside. All pale wood and brushed aluminium, with arty photographs of the royal family for decoration. Staff looking trendy and slightly sinister in black, with the pub name on their shirts. The new image seemed to be working: the lunchtime crowd was starting to thin out, but the bar was still busy with people trying to knock back another quick one before they returned to work.

I had been thinking of a pie and a pint, or perhaps a cheese sandwich. In fact, thinking about it, I quite fancied a cheese sandwich. Some mature cheddar on soft white bread with a bit of pickle. However, when I finally got sight of a menu, it had been subjected to the same upgrade as everything else. The pint was still on – though from some specialized microbrewery I'd never heard of – but pies were off, and the traditional cheese sandwich was now a ciabatta with mozzarella.

You've got to move with the times. I took it over to the least crowded corner I could find, and perched on a bar stool next to an old bloke with a pint and a morose expression.

"They've done this place up a bit," I said, trying to be sociable.

"Aye," he agreed, not looking at me. He was staring into his drink as if it were the last he'd ever have and it had curdled. Not in the mood for conversation, it seemed. Fair enough. I had things to think about myself, like whether or not Mickey Fayden's suspicions about this place had been right, and whether ciabatta should be this hard to chew. The pint, however, was quite good. I sipped at it, looking round, trying to visualize Laney in here scoring some Lappies.

Somehow, I couldn't make her fit the scenario. There was no solid evidence that she had come in here, though the logic pointed that way. Could she have been drugged against her will? Without her knowledge, even?

But that shouldn't have caused her to deliberately take her own life. La Paz might have taken away any fear or sense of danger, but from what June had told me, it wouldn't have made her suicidal.

I took out the Black Gull poem and read it through again, though it was already well engrained in my memory. Had she sat at one of these tables, writing these words, perhaps while she waited for the pills to take effect? Writing on this actual piece of paper?

"Been coming here thirty year, nigh on."

I glanced up from the poem, my chain of thought broken. "What?"

"Thirty year." The old chap hadn't shifted his gaze, but seemed to be replying to me. "Live just round the corner, don't I." It wasn't a question.

"So this is your local, then?"

"Aye. For thirty year. Used to be a nice quiet place too. Now look at it!" He jerked his head at the rest of the pub. It was already much quieter than it had been when I'd entered, but there were enough late lunchers to make his point.

"I suppose that's what they have to do to stay profitable," I suggested. "Move with the times, bring in the customers."

Making money was no excuse in his eyes. His snort of derision was loud enough to attract a glance from one of the staff, who had started collecting glasses from the vacated tables.

"Ain't a proper pub any more," he grumbled into his pint. "Not since that furrinner took over and changed everything."

"Foreigner?"

"Flamin' Spaniard. Changed the inside, changed the outside, changed the name, and even changed the flippin' beer!"

DAY 8: THE BEGINNING

The new beer wasn't bad, I thought, taking a sip of mine, but I didn't want to get into that argument. Instead, I took the opportunity to confirm what I'd thought about the name. "Used to be the King William, didn't it?"

"Aye, that's right." My companion finally raised his eyes from his drink, and looked at me. "'Ere, do I know you?"

"Shouldn't think so. I haven't been here before." I took a big gulp from my beer. "Well, I'd better get going. Nice to meet you."

"I've seen you in the paper, 'aven't I?"

"No, mate. Wrong bloke." I took a last drink and decided to abandon the rest, along with the ciabatta. This was the last place I wanted to be recognized.

"Yeah, you are him!" The old man was getting louder in his excitement. "You're the bloke who killed that poet! Knocked her down!"

It suddenly felt as if every eye in the room had turned towards me. Imagination, of course, but the lad from the bar, back with a tray for more empties, was certainly looking my way.

"Got to go." I stood up, but he put his hand out and grabbed my arm.

"She was here, you know. The poet lady. Same day it happened."

I paused, torn between my need to get away and my desire to confirm Laney's presence here. "Are you sure about that? Laney Grey was here?"

"Aye. Like I said. Sat just over there…" He nodded at a table nearby – the one that had just been cleared. "She was scribbling in her notebook. Then she tore the page out and put it in her pocket. Page like that one you've got there." He looked pointedly at the sheet of notepaper in my hand.

I quickly stuffed it in my pocket. "What did she do then?"

"Just got up and walked out. I thought she'd be coming back, because she left her bag an' her notebook – still open on the table, pen with it an' all. Even left her drink – just a coke, I think it was, but she'd hardly touched it." He shook his head in bemusement,

113

struggling with the concept of leaving a drink unfinished. "Anyhow, she didn't come back, and after a while I said about it to the bloke behind the bar. Because she'd left her stuff, hadn't she. Might have a purse in the bag, and you can't trust folks nowadays, can you? Was a time when you could leave your wallet on the table and it'd still be there when you came back for it. Now, you can't look the other way without some thieving git nicking off you. Everything's changed." He looked around sadly. In his eyes the change of décor and the increase in dishonesty were connected.

"What happened to the bag, then?"

"The barman called his boss. The Spanish bloke. And he got a right strop on when he heard what had happened. Sent some of his lads off to look for her. Kept asking me where she'd gone. I didn't have a clue and I told him. Wanted to know about the notebook and the torn page and what she'd written on it, but I couldn't help him with that. So the lads came back – couldn't find her. Then one of them comes in all panicked and says there's been an accident. So the boss took the bag and the notebook, and disappeared into the back. When he came out he was all smiling and friendly, drinks on the house, but I should keep it to myself what I'd seen. Bad for business, he said."

Bad for business, certainly, but which business? The pub, or the trade in La Paz? Canoso's thinking was obvious. He'd already had the police round once. He didn't want to give them any excuse to come back. But with Laney's bag hidden away, the only proof she'd been here at all was the old man's word, and he had been persuaded to keep quiet. Perhaps not a strong witness either, especially as all the staff would deny that Laney had ever been there. Mickey Fayden might suspect that she had, but he'd need something stronger than suspicion to get another search warrant.

"Interesting story. Sorry – what's your name?"

"Ed. Ed Bramley. Like the apple."

"Well, thanks for telling me, Ed. But I've got to go now. Here, have a drink on me." I slipped him a fiver.

114

"Thanks, lad. You know what? I never believed the things they said about you in the paper."

"You shouldn't believe anything you read in the paper," I said, but he'd already knocked back his pint and was heading to the bar for a refill.

The place was nearly empty now. Nobody was taking any notice of me, although the barman had shot a glance in my direction. No need to panic. The police needed to know what I knew about Laney. Not that I wanted to help Fayden out, but the sooner he got something concrete, the sooner he'd be off my back. And I might be able to do June a favour as well, in return for what she had done for me.

I stepped out of the door, turned back towards the Plaza, and called her number as I was walking. Got her voicemail. I stopped outside the wide window and looked in as I spoke, thinking carefully about what I should and shouldn't say. Ed was back in his favourite place with a fresh pint, which he raised in my direction when he saw me. I waved back, and continued slowly on my way, still talking.

"June. Hi, it's Rob. Rob Seaton. I've just heard something you might be interested in. I've just been talking to an old bloke named Ed Bramley. Apparently, he lives near the Prince William pub. Used to be the King William. Anyhow, he was drinking in there the day Laney died." No need to mention that I'd met him there. "He saw her in there, just before it happened. And you might want to talk to Sandra Deeson at the library. She had a letter – well, a poem actually – from Laney, posted the same day. I think she probably sent it from the post office in the Plaza. Um – well, I've got some ideas on that. Perhaps I can meet you sometime and talk about it? Not a date, of course! Well, bye then."

I hung up wondering where that last bit had come from. I'd honestly had no intention of arranging to meet her when I started talking.

Someone stepped in front of me. One of the bar staff.

"Boss wants a word with you," he said.

"Sorry, I'm in a hurry." I tried to step round him, and was grabbed from behind.

"Hey…" I began a protest, but I'd already been hustled through a side gate and into the back yard of the Prince William. The back hadn't had the same makeover as the front. I had a brief glimpse of stained concrete, crumbling brickwork, a parked white van, then I was shoved through a door, down a flight of steps, and into a sort of cellar. Whitewashed bricks, metal pipes covering one wall, stacked crates and barrels. And a man about my age. Dark hair, dark skin, white shirt, and an enigmatic expression.

He nodded at the men holding me, and they let go of my arms, stepping aside as he moved forward.

"I am Mateo Canoso." There was only the faintest trace of an accent in his voice. He looked more Spanish than he sounded. "And you are the bastard who killed my sister."

"Look, I'm truly sorry, but it was an accid –"

He punched me hard in the stomach.

Like most blokes, I'd always reckoned I could take care of myself in a fight. Would be pretty useful in fact, if it came to it. I didn't get a chance to prove it. He was too fast and too strong. Before I even saw it coming I was doubled up and collapsing to the floor, gasping desperately for breath. I was grabbed from either side before I could hit the ground, and hauled upright.

"I know it was an accident," Canoso said softly. "This is not important. But that she was my sister – this is the thing that is important."

He hit me again. He took his time about it, making sure that this time I saw it coming. I couldn't do anything about it; just hung there while he drove his fist into the side of my face.

"It is good that you have come here," he continued. "I would have come to find you eventually. But this is more convenient."

I could taste blood.

"Thank you for that." He hit me again, kept on hitting me,

116

body and face, but it was hard to tell where through the red agony that overwhelmed me.

After a while it stopped. There were hands going through my pockets, taking my phone, my wallet, my keys. My watch from my wrist. There was talking. Questions. A sudden splash of cold water over my face that brought me back to awareness.

"I asked you something! Who did you call?"

"What?" I gasped.

"The call you made as you were leaving. This was seen. So, you will tell me now who it was that you called. Who did you speak to?"

"I..." It was hard to think with the pain. "June... I was calling June."

"Who is June?"

Even in my befuddled state, "police officer" seemed like the wrong answer. "She's my girlfriend."

"What did you speak of to her?"

"I was making a date."

One of Canoso's little helpers had been fiddling with my phone. I was still using the old one, and hadn't got round to locking the screen. Not that I'd have kept the pin number from them if they'd asked.

"Last number dialled was another mobile," he announced.

"Call it again," Canoso ordered.

I started to understand what was going on. They were trying to find out if I'd called the police. I couldn't remember if June's voicemail message announced her as a police officer. I didn't think so. It was her personal number, not a work phone. But what if she answered it herself? Would she say PC Henshaw or just June Henshaw?

"Voicemail," he announced. "It's the right name."

".Good. So you tell the truth, Mr Seaton." I was slumped on the floor, though I didn't remember getting there. Canoso grabbed my hair and dragged my head up. "Keep going. Tell me where you got this." He was waving a piece of paper in front of me.

I struggled to focus on it; a task made more difficult because my right eye wouldn't open properly. But I could make out handwriting in blue ink.

"Laney's poem," I muttered.

He jerked harder on my hair, sending additional waves of pain crashing round my skull. "This I know. I asked where you got it."

Behind me, a door opened and closed. Something was tossed onto the floor next to me.

"There's her bag. The notebook's inside."

My head was released. With an effort, I kept it up. In front of me, Canoso was emptying the contents of a large handbag onto the floor. My vision was still slightly fuzzy, but there didn't seem anything out of the ordinary. A purse, in the same buff leather as the handbag. Make-up, keys, some tissues. A small bottle of water, half empty. Pens. Quite a few pens. A diary, and a notebook: A5, same size as the torn sheet.

He opened it, flicked through, found a place, and laid the sheet in it. "Ah. It is the missing page," he said. "And nothing on it except one of her poems."

"Guess we can relax, then?" The man sounded relieved.

"I think so. It seems that my sister left no loose ends. No suicide note, no cry for help, no message to the police. Just poetry."

"Was it just an accident, then?"

"Who knows? She had taken La Paz. I thought this was to make her suicide easier, but perhaps she had not intended to kill herself. Maybe with the stuff in her, she just forgot to care. A huge inconvenience! Her contacts, they would have been useful for our distribution. And just when I'd got her to see sense, as well. But it is of no matter. We will find other couriers, other routes."

"What about him?"

"Ah, yes. The van driver." Canoso turned back to me. "Now this does seem curious. This very same man who killed my sister, now he comes into my place with paper from her notebook! Please explain this to me."

118

DAY 8: THE BEGINNING

"Got it from the library," I mumbled. It was hard to talk properly. One whole side of my face felt swollen.

Canoso sighed, shook his head, and kicked me very hard in my side. "A stupid lie," he said. "This is not from any printed book. It did not come from a library. Try again."

"The librarian was a friend of hers," I gasped.

Canoso frowned.

"No, please, it's true!" I was desperate to avoid another kick. I'd felt something crack inside me the last time and now it hurt to breathe. "She ran Laney's website for her. Laney posted the poem to her; must have been just before she died."

Canoso was still frowning, but he kept his feet on the floor. "And why did she give it to you?"

"I've been reading Laney's poems. To try to find out about her. After what happened, I wanted to… to… know about her. So the librarian lent me that – Laney's last poem. Thought it might help."

He nodded. "Ah. Perhaps this is the truth. But why did you come here with it?"

"I was walking around. Seeing where it happened. Hadn't been back since… came in here for a pint and a bite, that's all. Didn't know about you being related. Didn't know she'd ever been here."

There was a long pause. I hoped he believed me. I hoped desperately that he believed me. It was hard to think with the pain. If he started kicking me again I wouldn't be able to come up with any more lies. It might all come out then: all that I knew about Laney and La Paz and the police. I really didn't want Canoso to know that I knew all that.

He shrugged. "Well, this is of no importance." Canoso turned away from me. "Go and speak with the old man. Give him plenty to drink and make sure he knows to keep his mouth shut."

"No problem. He'll be bladdered before he leaves anyway; probably won't remember much."

"Yes, that is what should happen. I will need to change my

119

shirt – this one has blood on it. Then I'm going to the library. If this story is true, then we are in the clear and can start production again, but I need to make a few arrangements. If it is not, then our guest will explain things to me once more."

He kicked me as he said it. Not hard, just emphasizing his point, but it sent a new burst of pain through me and brought out a strange noise. Something between a scream and a groan. A distant part of me wondered at it.

"What do we do with him for now?"

"Leave him here. He will go nowhere. As for later, that is one of the things I will arrange."

There were footsteps, more conversation. A door slammed, and I was left in silence.

For a while, I just lay still. As long as I didn't move and kept my breathing shallow, the pain was bearable. As long as they didn't come back, I was OK.

But they would come back. Canoso would come back.

The library would confirm my story, I was sure of that. If he told Sandra he was Laney's brother, she'd tell him all about it. There was no reason why she shouldn't. I hoped desperately that she would tell him everything, without reservation. Not that he would hurt her – would he? Not in a public place like a library. But now I knew what Canoso was capable of...

No, he would have no need to hurt Sandra. She'd tell him everything he wanted to know. And then he'd make his arrangements for me. The pain was still fogging my head, but I didn't need to think very hard to understand what that meant. He wasn't about to let me go; not after beating me half to death. His arrangements probably involved some wet concrete and a building site, or perhaps a deep lake and a few weights.

People might look for me, of course. Colin would check my flat after a while, might report me missing. Perhaps June would look round a bit. Mickey would want to know where I'd gone, for his own reasons. But even if they tracked me to the Prince William, even if they spoke to Ed and he was sober enough to remember me, what would that prove? I came in, had a drink, left again. I'd been snatched off the street so quickly that even I hadn't realized what was happening until it had happened. If anyone had seen it, they wouldn't remember.

Laney's bag was still on the floor in front of me, contents strewn round it. The notebook lay open, with the torn-out page next to it. Canoso must have been really worried by it – not knowing what she had written, or who she'd sent it to. Now that loose end was cleared up, things were looking good for him. Bad for me, though.

It was fear that got me moving again. I forced myself to sit up. Some of the pain wasn't too bad now. It was the way it hurt to breathe that really worried me.

My stuff had been dumped on the floor with hers – wallet and keys and the other things taken from my pockets. But not my phone; they'd kept that. I picked them up, checked my wallet. They hadn't even bothered to rob me.

Laney would have had a mobile phone. Did she leave it in her bag or take it with her? I rummaged through the bag and contents without success. Of course it wouldn't be that easy; they wouldn't just leave it there for me.

I carefully got to my feet and went across to the door, trying to breathe as lightly as possible all the way. Obviously, it was locked. What was more, it was faced with a metal sheet that would need some heavy-duty power tools to break through. There wasn't a handle, or even a keyhole. So I had no chance of picking the lock – even if I'd known how to do it.

There was a keypad inset into the wall next to it. Numbers one to nine, plus zero. They had something similar on the warehouse door at work. It needed four digits in the correct order. The bloke who'd installed it told me that there were ten thousand possible combinations, so I wasn't likely to stumble across it by chance.

Nevertheless, I punched in four zeros, hoping that it might have been left on the factory setting. The LED stayed stubbornly red and the door remained firm. I hadn't really expected anything else.

I had a brief fantasy about forcing off the cover and rewiring the electronics. But quite apart from the fact that that was something else I didn't know how to do, the keypad was deeply recessed into the wall, and inaccessible without proper tools.

I glanced round the room, looking for something I could use. Not to get out, but perhaps to attract attention, get help. The pile of plastic crates and empty beer barrels didn't seem promising. I could try banging on the door with a barrel, but the most likely people to hear would be Canoso's lads. And in any case, the way I felt I'd struggle just to lift one of them.

That also took out the possibility of using them as weapons, or of setting up elaborate obstacles. I had fantasy visions of Canoso and his lads tripping over strategically placed barrels, giving me the chance to make my escape while they floundered. But the chances of that actually working were somewhere between improbable and impossible. And shifting enough barrels to construct a decent trap would be likely to finish me off, saving Canoso the trouble.

The pain in my chest wasn't going away. The kick in my side might have cracked or broken a rib. I had frightening thoughts of jagged bones puncturing my lungs; of drowning in my own blood. Nevertheless, I staggered over to the barrels. There really wasn't anything else to look at. Perhaps there might be something behind the pile.

I pulled on a barrel, and the pain spiked. Even empty, it was too much for me to cope with in my present condition. A ceiling-high pile of plastic crates offered more hope. I gave one of them a tentative pull. They had not been stacked too carefully. My one small tug set the whole stack wobbling. A crate toppled, and suddenly they were all clattering and crashing down around me. Around me and on top of me. A corner impacted my ear and I dropped to my knees. When I looked up again, I was facing a king.

He was dusty and a little faded, but still impressive. Wearing some sort of military uniform from a past century, he struck a heroic pose and looked out across the cellar with regal disdain. In case there was any doubt as to his identity, his name was written below: King William.

So this was where the pub's former identity was hidden. The old king, buried down here to make way for the new prince.

> *Deep in the grave of a forgotten past,*
> *Once resplendent for all to see,*
> *Now cast down, its glory tarnished.*

Laney's words came back to me. Like all her writing, it seemed so cryptic till you saw what she meant. Then it was so vividly clear that you wondered how you could have missed it.

The implications set the back of my neck tingling. Laney had been here, in this cellar, perhaps in this exact spot, and had seen exactly what I was now seeing. Which meant that this was the Black Gull's nest. The place where it laid its poisonous eggs.

But where, exactly? There was nothing here but crates and barrels. If Canoso had been making or storing La Paz here, there was no sign of it now. He must have cleared the place after the police raid. Though if it had been after, then surely Fayden's team would have found something? Hard to believe that they would have overlooked the cellar. Perhaps they had come too late, after the merchandise had already been moved on.

And had Laney written "Black Gull" before the raid, then? That was possible, but I'd assumed that she'd scribbled down the words just before she went to carry out her suicide. They seemed to have that immediacy to them; a sense of something happening now.

Looking for further inspiration, I went back to her bag and picked up the crumpled sheet. As I did so, I remembered the bag being dumped on the floor – by someone who had come out of a door behind me. But there was only one door in the room, and I'd been facing it.

I looked at the wall that had been behind me. It appeared solid enough, the same brickwork as the others, only this one wasn't whitewashed, probably because of the metal pipes that ran all over it. They were a dull silver in colour, except around some of the joints, which looked rusty. I'd noticed the pipes when they hustled me in. I'd seen similar arrangements in pubs before, part of the pump system that delivered beer on tap to the bar. These didn't appear to be in use. They weren't connected to anything that I could see. Perhaps they were part of the old system from the King William days.

Or perhaps they were something else. I read Laney's original words again, to check my memory.

Secure behind an armoured web.

The mesh of pipes could be seen as a web. And metal pipes would make it an armoured web.

I went over to the wall and examined it as closely as I could with one eye. There were no obvious cracks in the brickwork, no neat door outline, no convenient breaks in the pipes. I pushed, pulled, and swore at likely places, all without effect. If I hadn't remembered the door opening, I wouldn't have believed it was there. As it was, I was doubting myself. Laney had it right…

Which does not,
yield,

But what else had she said? I looked at the poem again.

Save to the knowing hand,
That which is empty.

The knowing hand would obviously be the hand that knew how to open the door. That didn't help much. And what was in an empty hand? Nothing? What did she mean by that?

Nothing – as in zero? Nought? A number on a keypad, for example? There was no keypad on the wall. But there was one by the other door. And just because it was over there, there was no reason why it shouldn't control something over here.

I went back across the room, trying to remember if anyone had been standing here when the wall opened, but I hadn't been paying much attention at the time.

If those strangely structured four lines were actually a code, then the most obvious way to read it was by counting the words. So… "Which does not" was three. "Yield" would be one. "Save to the knowing hand", five. And "That which is empty" equalled four.

"Three, one, five, four." I spoke the numbers aloud as I pressed the buttons, a desperate incantation, because if it failed…

The LED remained red. I looked at the far wall, but nothing had changed. I swore. Laney had let me down. The poem was just a poem, nothing more. Like Canoso had said.

That didn't make sense though. The old pub sign, the "armoured web"… Laney had to have been here. If Canoso had bothered reading it properly, he'd have seen it as well. But it was "just poetry" to him. Which, I realized, was obviously why she'd done it like that. A final defence to hide her message from her brother.

So what was the message?

I read it again, and could have slapped myself, except that I was already hurting enough. I'd already worked out what "that which is empty" meant.

I tapped in another set of numbers: three, one, five, zero.

The LED turned green. Across the room, a section of wall, complete with attached pipes, slid smoothly and silently inwards before rotating off to one side. Beyond, bright fluorescent lighting flickered on.

I had no idea what a drugs factory would look like. It wasn't something I'd had previous experience of. The closet thing to it

I could think of was the science classroom at school, only with better equipment.

The room itself was easily three times larger than the cellar I had been in, though the walls were the same whitewashed brick. Long benches ran down either side, filled with shiny stainless steel and glass items. I recognized none of them, except for the pill press at one end and a laptop at the other.

At the far end of the room were piled drums and open packing crates, presumably the raw materials and the likely source of an acrid smell. I was relieved to see a door in the far wall. It made sense that Canoso would want another way out, but there was no guarantee of that. All my efforts so far might have done no more than enlarge my prison.

The centre of the room was occupied by a long table. In the middle of it, piles of plastic bags spilled from an opened cardboard box onto the table top. Small ones, with a resealable opening. The end of the table closest to me had a precarious mound of them, but these weren't empty.

I stepped into the room and went to the table for a closer look. Each sealed bag contained a pinkish-white capsule, about the size of a standard paracetamol. There must have been hundreds piled up on the table. More were stored underneath in a dozen plastic crates. At the far end of the table, several deep trays contained hundreds more pills, loose and waiting to be bagged. Each had a peace symbol on one side and the letters LP on the other.

"So this is La Paz," I said to myself.

I felt Laney's presence here, as though she were standing right next to me, her hand reaching out to take a tablet. Two tablets. Three, even. She raised them to her mouth and swallowed them, one after another, washing them down with the little bottle of water from her bag, which she had brought for the purpose. She gave me a look full of fear and despair and determination and courage, slowly fading to impassive calm as the drug gripped her. Then she walked out of the door, going up to the pub to write her final poem.

The few she'd taken would not have been missed from that pile. The stock-taking didn't appear to be rigorous.

In spite of the pain in my head, things were coming together for me. June had told me how La Paz had been distributed in Spain. Canoso had been annoyed because he couldn't use Laney to do the same here. Her access to schools and colleges and community centres was what he wanted to use. Of course Laney would refuse, but somehow he'd found a way to put pressure on her, bend her to his will. Until the only way out she could see was to step in front of my van.

It wasn't me who had killed her. It was Canoso.

The thought struck me with such power that I actually gasped. The guilt I'd felt had become familiar, so much a part of me that it didn't simply lift off me but was wrenched away. I'd told myself and had been told so many times that it wasn't my fault, to no effect. Realizing that it was someone else's fault freed me.

But that still left the question of why she hadn't simply gone to the police. Why did she not only have to kill herself but do everything she could to make it look like an accident? Why did she disguise her suicide note and the location of the drug factory in a poem?

I put the questions aside, along with the relief I felt. None of this changed my immediate situation: trapped, beaten half to death, and with a seriously nasty criminal coming back to finish the job at any time. Escape was the priority.

I turned to the door in the back wall. A perfectly ordinary door, unpainted wood and no lock. I turned the handle, the thought that it might just be a cupboard sending a new pulse of fear through me. But it opened onto a long, dimly lit brick corridor with a flight of stairs just visible at the far end. A way out! And to judge by the length of the passage, it couldn't be back into the pub. The cellar itself must run under the alley that bordered the Prince William, probably part of the original pub building and pre-dating the surrounding structures, perhaps by hundreds of years. The tunnel exit could well be in the next street along. Which suited me. The further away I could get the better.

But I paused before entering, to think. Once I got out of here, I planned to go straight to the police. But could I prove my story? Once Canoso discovered my escape, he'd start covering his tracks. If he sealed up the hidden door it might be hard to convince anyone. My tales of a secret drugs factory would sound like the ravings of a lunatic, especially as the place had already been thoroughly searched. I doubted if they'd break down the wall just on my word alone. They'd have to investigate the assault, but I had no proof that it had even taken place in the pub.

So I needed evidence. Fortunately there was plenty of that lying around. And this was probably the only chance I'd have to get it.

I returned to the first cellar, collected Laney's bag, and stuffed the contents back inside. Then I added a handful of Lappies in their plastic bags. On the way through I noticed a button next to the door, on the inside, and pressed it. The door obligingly shut itself. Of course, they'd soon realize where I'd gone, but there was no need to make it obvious.

I stopped by the trays of unbagged pills and wondered if taking one or two would help me, but quickly decided against it. Right now, I needed painkillers, not emotion suppressants. Fear of what Canoso might do when he came back was the only thing that kept me moving.

Shutting the door behind me, I went down the passage, up the stairs. The door at the end matched the one in the cellar: metal and securely locked. But with a promising-looking button next to it. To my great relief, it fulfilled its promise. The door swung open as smoothly as the one in the cellar had, and I stepped out into freedom.

My timing was lousy. As I stepped out, Mateo Canoso was about to step in.

The sudden opening of the door must have taken him by surprise, which was the thing that saved me. That and the fact that it opened outwards. If he'd been far enough back for it to miss him, I would have been dead.

As it was, he was directly in front of it when it began to move, perhaps reaching for a keypad next to it. It opened into his face and he stumbled backwards, arms flailing as he tried to keep his balance, and I had a bare second of advantage.

Adrenaline is amazing. I'd staggered slowly and painfully along the corridor, dragged myself up the stairs with teeth gritted against the pain. Now I charged out from the doorway like an Olympic sprinter, head down and straight into Canoso. There was a meaty thunk as my head smashed into his face. He went over backwards and I fell on top of him, my knee driving into his stomach as I did so. I scrambled back to my feet, while Canoso curled up gasping for breath.

"Yes, I know what that feels like," I told him. I was pleased to see his face covered in blood – at the very least, I'd split his lip. "You're going to have to change your shirt again," I added, looking round me. We were in a deserted yard, surrounded by high and featureless walls and lined with garages. A smart BMW – presumably Canoso's – was parked nearby, and just beyond was the exit: a solid-looking metal gate, topped with barbed wire, sliding smoothly closed.

"I…'ll… kill… you…" Canoso gasped.

"Like you weren't going to anyway!" I sneered, and ran for the exit. I didn't even take time for the goodbye kick I owed him – the thought of getting trapped inside with him had pumped up my adrenaline again, and I sprinted for the closing gap. Helpless he might be for the moment, but I didn't rate my chances of keeping him that way. All I needed to do was get outside and find a phone – or anyone with a mobile.

I slipped through the closing gap with a foot to spare, and looked round for help. The street curved gently away to left and right. In both directions it was deserted. On my side it was lined with blank walls topped with broken glass, and punctuated only by occasional doorways. On the opposite side was a fenced-off industrial wasteland – weeds growing in piles of broken brick and cracked concrete, a few walls still standing, windows gaping emptily.

I went right, towards the nearest doorway. Not sprinting now. I knew where I was. The locally infamous Delford Mills Reclamation Project. A huge Victorian factory, derelict for years and finally demolished with huge fanfare and extravagant promises of major development. Except that all the money had mysteriously disappeared, along with several senior members of the project. There was much outcry and many pointed fingers, but the money had never returned and the project remained officially "on hold". As part of that project, much of the surrounding area had also been scheduled for demolition and redevelopment. Streets and streets of grimy terraced housing had been cleared, boarded up, then left empty.

Laney had written a poem about it, making a vivid contrast between the bustling town centre and the deserted wasteland, less than half a mile apart. More importantly for my present situation, I wasn't going to find any help here. I wasn't going to find anyone.

I'd reached the first doorway. Its wood was old and weathered, it had no latch or handle, and probably hadn't been opened for years. Nevertheless, I hammered on it.

"Help! Open up! I need help!" My shouts sounded thin and hollow, disappearing traceless into the silence. The adrenaline was wearing off now. I was panting, every breath another stabbing pain. I could hear distant traffic, a dog barking, but nothing from behind the door.

A car started nearby. Very near. Looking back the way I'd come, the curve of the street enabled me to see the metal gate to the yard sliding open. Canoso would be after me in less than a minute. I looked round wildly. There was nowhere to hide on the street. But the chain-link fence opposite was broken down or torn open in several places.

DAY 8: THE BEGINNING

I forced myself to run again, pushed through the biggest hole I could see, with loose strands of wire tearing indiscriminately at skin and clothes, and scrambled up a pile of loose bricks, the scream of a car doing a hi-rev reverse in the background. It changed gear just as I flopped over the top of the pile, and accelerated along the street as I half rolled, half slid down the opposite slope.

It went past, engine noise fading, which meant that Canoso hadn't seen me, but he wouldn't have to go far before realizing he'd overshot. Then he'd search in the other direction, but only for a short distance. After that, he'd know which way I'd gone.

I was in agony, but I had to keep moving, had to lose myself in the wasteland before he started searching for me. I put aside the pain, forced myself to ignore it, and headed deeper into the ruins.

The car came back up the street, and went past, searching in the other direction. I felt a vague satisfaction at having predicted that. If I could outguess him, I could stay hidden. If I could survive until it got dark, I might have a chance to get away. I wasn't sure how long that would be. Without my watch or phone, I had no idea what time it was. Even the sun was hidden behind a hard white veil of cloud. Nonetheless, it was a warm day. I was sweating and gasping for breath, going slower.

There was no telling where Canoso would enter the project from. He could come through the fence almost anywhere; he could be approaching from any direction. I had to find better cover than the random piles of rubble in this area – perhaps where the walls were still standing? Getting there, however, meant crossing a more open stretch, patches of grass breaking through crumbling asphalt. I felt my exposure. At any moment, I'd hear Canoso shout. Or perhaps I'd just hear his footsteps.

It wasn't more than a hundred yards. It felt like a mile before I collapsed, panting, next to a wall. It wasn't good enough. I was still too visible. But further along, another upright section formed a right angle, and a few first-floor beams remained intact, giving at least the illusion of security. More rubble screened off the corner, making for an even better hiding place. I hauled myself upright again, and used the wall for support as I moved towards it.

As I came closer, it became obvious that I wasn't the first person to see the possibilities there. The bricks across the corner weren't a random pile – someone had placed them there in a crude wall. Sheets of dirty plastic had been draped across the first-floor beams to provide a roof.

So not all local residents had moved out. I crept up cautiously in case anyone was at home. But also hopefully, since even tramps had mobile phones nowadays. Peering through the gap that served as a front door, I found the premises vacant, though there was evidence of occupancy, mostly in the form of empty plastic bottles and lager cans. Two litres of cheap cider seemed to be the drink of choice, and the discards were piled knee-deep in the far corner. There were smaller piles of cigarette ends and empty packets, along with the occasional fast food wrapper, all arranged round the only piece of furniture: a filthy mattress.

The smell was worse than the sight. The main component was human waste product, with undertones of booze and ash. A blackened area in the middle of the floor was probably the main source of that.

"Look, they've even got central heating," I said to myself. But the attempt at humour failed to get any response, even from me. Holding my breath, I went inside.

A flat slab of concrete stuck out of the makeshift wall that blocked most of the corner from sight. Not much of a seat, but anything was better than standing up for a moment longer. Laying down would have been preferable, but there wasn't much space to stretch out – apart from on the mattress, and I wasn't yet so far gone that I'd even touch that, let alone lay on it. Sitting up also had the advantage of keeping my head where I could breathe relatively fresh air. Even so, the stench was incredible. I concentrated on breathing through my mouth. Actually, I didn't have much choice, since half my nose seemed to be blocked. Probably with blood, if it wasn't broken. Hard to tell, with my whole face throbbing. It said something for the strength of the smell that it still got through.

I settled back against the broken masonry, trying to find a more comfortable position. Laney would have found the right word to describe the stink, I thought. Something like "miasma", for example. I'd come across that in one of her poems. Not a word I'd ever have thought of otherwise. I looked around me again, wondering where the usual resident was. Probably out begging, or buying another bottle of rotgut to drink himself to sleep with.

I let my eyes drift shut. Laney would have had a lot to say about this place, I thought, and not just the smell. She'd have thought past that. She'd have found a way to describe it, and show the squalor. But beyond that, she'd have made people see the sadness of it, the loneliness of a man sitting in the ruins drinking himself to death. An abandoned person in an abandoned landscape.

I pictured her sitting next to me, taking her notebook out of her bag, beginning to write. She glanced up and met my gaze with a smile. Then she looked at what she'd written, and switched to a frown.

"What's wrong?" I asked her.

She held up the notebook to show me: *"You're not safe here."*

I jerked awake, twisting round and trying to look in every direction at once. Nothing had changed. But she was right. Or my subconscious was, at any rate. I might be hidden from view here, but it was too obvious a hiding place. Once Canoso realized that I wasn't wandering around in the open, he'd start looking into corners like this. And if he found me here, I'd be trapped. Plenty of places to hide a body. Just shovel enough bricks over me and I'd disappear. Forever, perhaps, or at least until they actually got round to the redevelopment. Which would be about the same time.

I crept out, wary as a rabbit, and feeling horribly exposed – though also glad of the fresher air. There was no movement out in the wasteland, no sound but distant traffic.

No more running. I didn't have it in me. Now I was in stealth mode, slipping along the wall and then cautiously out among the rubble heaps. Like a ninja, I thought. A knackered ninja, with busted ribs, carrying a woman's bag. Well, why not? Who said I had to conform to the stereotype?

My thoughts were wandering, my head felt light. Full of blood and air and the worst ache I could remember.

"Focus!" I told myself. *And shut up*, I added mentally, realizing I'd spoken aloud.

I came to another wall. At least, I hoped it was another wall, otherwise I was going in circles. This one seemed lower. I followed it, reminding myself to be careful, to be quiet.

A good thing too. As I came near the end of the wall, I heard voices.

I stopped moving. Almost stopped breathing. I couldn't make out the words, but it sounded like three of them. None of them were Canoso.

I moved cautiously further along the wall, testing each step. The voices got louder, and I started making out individual words. They were talking about football. The local team were useless. Not a single decent player among them. It was the manager's fault. He was useless. They weren't talking about me, which meant that they weren't looking for me. Not Canoso's voice, not Canoso's men.

I reached the end of the standing section of the wall, and risked a quick peek round the edge. There were indeed three of them, sitting on a collection of old car seats about ten feet away. None looking in my direction, fortunately. They were all wearing hoodies – black, grey, and blue – so I couldn't see much of them, but they seemed quite young. Teenagers. Sixteen or seventeen at the most. They were drinking out of cans and smoking. Not tobacco – even through my badly abused nose I could smell that. I could hear them better now. The topic had switched to girls, and they were comparing pictures on their phones.

If they had phones, they could call the police for me.

I stepped from behind the wall. "Hi," I called. It came out as a croak, but loud enough that they all turned to look at me. There was an outburst of expletive-laden surprise that could be summarized as: "Who are you and where did you come from?"

I went towards them, coughed, and tried again. "Hi."

They were all standing up now, staring at me with a mixture of shock and curiosity. Their initial reaction was to hide their smokes behind their back, but as it became clear that I was on my own – and didn't look like a copper – they brought them out again.

"You look like hell! What happened to you?" That was Grey Hoodie, who was a bit bigger, perhaps a bit older, than the others.

"Ran into some trouble; got a bit of a kicking. Need some help."

They looked at each other, then back at me. "No kidding?" asked Blue Hoodie, who I could now see was a thin-faced lad with bad acne.

"Who did it?" That was the third one, Black Hoodie, a pudgy guy with glasses. He glanced round apprehensively as he spoke, as if expecting to be attacked himself.

"Some blokes in a pub," I told him. Which was actually the truth.

Grey Hoodie had a flat face and square jaw, and was gazing with interest at Laney's bag, which I was carrying on my shoulder. "Nice handbag. Is it yours?"

"No." The last thing I needed was for them to think I was gay. They didn't look like politically correct people.

"Must'a nicked it then," said Black Hoodie. "That why you got a smacking?"

"No, I didn't nick it." I was struggling to think. I needed a good explanation. "It's my girlfriend's."

"You always walk round with your girlfriend's handbag?" one of them said, and they all laughed.

"I reckon he's a poofter," Grey Hoodie added. There was a nasty glint in his eye. I suspected that he'd welcome the chance to beat up a gay. Or anyone else that looked like an easy target. Just then, I was an easy target, but it would be fatal to let them know how easy. Ignoring the pain, I pulled myself up to my full height, which was significantly taller than any of the three hoodies, and glared down at Grey. I was pretty sure he was the leader.

"Get lost!" I told him. "My girlfriend left it in the pub. I went back to get it and found some blokes going through it. So we had a few words, didn't we? And I got the bag back, but they went and got some mates and it turned a bit nasty." Best story I could come up with on the spur of the moment.

They looked at each other again, and back at me, obviously weighing up their chances. I was on my own and had already been beaten up once – but I was also bigger than any of them. They could probably take me, but not without getting hurt in the process. At least, that was the impression I hoped to convey. I glared at them, trying to show that I'd had quite enough nonsense for one day and I wasn't about to take any more. Especially, I glared at Grey, making it clear that if it hit the fan, he'd be the first to get a smack in the kisser.

"So how did you end up out here, then?" he asked. It was a slight step back from confrontation, though he was still probing my story.

"There were a dozen of them, so I had to leg it." They would assume that a dozen was an exaggeration, but if they reduced that by fifty per cent, it was still an impressive number and sufficient to justify a retreat. "Ducked in here and shook them off, but I need to get out again. My phone got lost in all the aggro, so I need to borrow one, get some help."

"What sort of help? Who d'yer want to call?"

I wanted to call the police, but I was getting the impression that they wouldn't go along with that idea, and suggesting it would probably put them back in favour of giving me a good kicking.

"My girlfriend. She'll come and pick me up." Hopefully in a car with flashing blue lights.

Grey gave me a long look. "Suppose I lend you my phone, then. What's in it for me?"

The chance to be a good neighbour? The opportunity to cross "good deed for the day" off your checklist? Somehow, I didn't think that these would be motivating factors. I went for something more basic.

I dug out my wallet, pulled out a fiver. "There you go."

Grey snorted. "Five quid? Are you having a laugh?"

"What do you mean? A fiver for letting me use your phone for a minute?" I was genuinely indignant.

"Yeah, but you're the one who needs a phone, ain't yer?"

"OK. Here's another. Ten quid, and that's a rip off. I could buy a phone for that!"

"Not out here, you couldn't!" Grey pointed out. "And those blokes are still looking for you, ain't they?" He eyed my wallet with interest, obviously wondering how much more cash I had on me.

The answer was: none at all. I opened it up and showed him. "That's it. Ten quid or forget it."

He hesitated, looking at it, looking at me.

"Come on. It's the easiest tenner you'll make in your life."

"All right, then." He reached out for the money, but I pulled my hand back.

"Phone first."

He glared at me, but held out the phone. This time, though, he was the one to pull back. "You're not calling the coppers, are you?" he asked suspiciously. "Only they record all their calls, don't they? I don't want them knowing my number."

"I'm not calling the coppers," I promised him. Just one copper, actually, but he didn't need to know that. "Just my girlfriend. If you like, I'll give you the number and you can dial it, OK? And I'll tell her to delete it. No record." I held up the money again, and he stared at it greedily.

"So tell me the number, then."

I repeated June's mobile number slowly, digit by digit – wondering in the back of my mind why I had found it so easy to remember her number when I'd never memorized anyone else's. Not the time to go there.

"OK, it's ringing." He handed it over, and I swapped it for the ten quid.

I had a sudden fear that it might go to voicemail again, but she picked up almost at once.

"Who is this?"

"June – it's me. Rob."

"Rob? Dammit, you shouldn't keep calling me! I told you that. Especially now, when I'm at work!"

"Yes, I know, but listen, please – I'm in a bit of trouble."

The Three Hoodies were showing a little too much interest in the conversation, and were edging closer as they did so. I took a step away and turned my back, hoping they'd get that it was a private matter.

June sighed. "I might have known. What sort of trouble, Rob? And make it quick. I am on duty, you know."

"Yes, I'm sorry – but did you get that message I left earlier?"

"Yes, I got it, but I haven't had time to do anything about it. I'll get back to you on that, OK?"

"Yes – I mean no! Don't hang up! There's been a development… I was at the Prince William. That's where I met the old bloke I told you about."

"You went to the Prince William? To Canoso's pub? You moron!"

"Yes, you're probably right. But the thing is, I had a bit of a – a confrontation. With Canoso. And it got a bit physical… I got away, but he's after me now."

"A confrontation? Are you hurt?"

I was pleased to hear some concern in her voice. "A bit. But I really need some help, June." The hoodies had ignored my right to privacy, and were crowding close, listening intently. "I can't say too

138

much. But I found out a few things that he won't want me talking about." I took another step away from the gang, and lowered my voice. "Regarding what we talked about – you know."

"La Paz?" A sharper interest came into her voice, overlying the concern. Professional reaction.

"Yes. Exactly that. I have some –" I was about to say "evidence", but the hoodies were crowding me again, and they might not like that word – "... stuff you'd be interested in."

"Right. Where are you?"

"Delford Mills."

"The project? That's a big area. Whereabouts, exactly?"

"I don't know. Somewhere in the middle of it."

"Oh, great. OK, I'm on my way. Try and get over to Gladstone Street. I'll come down there."

"Which one's Gladstone Street?"

"It runs down the east side of the demolition site."

"Which way's east?" I had lost all sense of direction. The sun still wasn't visible, and I had no idea how to navigate with it anyway. I'm Generation Sat-Nav.

"Never mind. Just look for a street with a lot of boarded-up houses next to it. I'll be there ASAP."

"OK. Thanks, June."

"Stay safe."

She broke the connection, and I offered the phone back to Grey Hoodie, who snatched it quickly. There was a strange look in his eyes; in all their eyes.

"You didn't say it was Canoso who was after you!" he blurted out, and from the tone of his voice I identified the look in his eyes. It was fear.

"Yeah, well, it's my problem, not yours," I told him.

"If that Spanish git finds out we helped you..." Blue Hoodie began. He was backing off from me as if I'd turned radioactive.

"Listen – you never saw us, right?" Grey was also backing off. Black was already legging it.

"Right, OK, no problem. But – just a minute – which way's Gladstone Street?"

"You're a dead man!" Grey shouted, then turned and ran, with Blue close behind him.

It seemed they'd heard of Canoso.

I started to follow them, hoping that they were heading for Gladstone Street. The pain was as bad as ever, but I was re-energized by hope. June was on her way. I was nearly safe.

There was a faint path, winding through a patch of weeds. It took me out into the open again, and my skin crawled with apprehension, but I followed it anyway. It must have been the way the hoodies had come in, so offered the best chance of getting out. I looked round at every step and kept stopping to listen. Nothing moved. The only sound was my breathing. *Long may it continue,* I thought, and moved on.

The path took me to yet another crumbling wall, which gave me some cover again. I followed the wall until another huge pile of broken masonry loomed up in front of me. It was too high to climb in my present state. Left was blocked by the wall, which had grown to a substantial height. So it was right, then, though that would take me back into a more open area. I looked around again, listened. Still no movement, no new sounds. Right it was.

I was stumbling more. It was such an effort to keep lifting my feet over the uneven surface, and I had to keep looking at the ground just in front of me; not thinking about where I was going, just trying to keep moving.

It was a shock when the ground disappeared. I was so far gone by then that I nearly stepped over the edge before I realized it. As it was, I snapped out of my stupor and found myself teetering over a twenty-foot drop.

It had probably been a cellar at one time, or perhaps the base for some vast piece of Victorian engineering. A huge square hole in the ground, about forty feet on each side, as far as I could tell. The mound I'd been following carried on into the pit, filling half of it.

And on the other side there were houses. They didn't look occupied. The windows and doors were covered with metal sheets. It was still part of the project; they just hadn't got round to demolishing it yet. It had to be Gladstone Street.

I struggled to get my breath under control, and felt relief welling up. I'd made it! I just needed to get round this pit, then across another short stretch of wasteland, find a hole in the fence and I'd be out.

Above me there was a rattling of bricks. I looked up at the top of the mound. Grinning down at me was a beefy young man dressed in black. The last time I'd seen him had been in the cellar beneath the Prince William. He had a gun in his hand, and was pointing it at me.

"There you are!" He was red faced and sweaty, the climb up to the top of the mound having been a tough one. "You stand still, or I'll put a bullet in you!" He pulled out a phone with his free hand and speed-dialled. "I've got him!" he announced, loud enough for me to hear at the bottom of the mound. "He's over by the big pit on the far side. No, he's not going anywhere."

I was, though. As soon as he started talking, I took a step backwards.

"I said stand still! Are you stupid, or what? This is a gun I'm pointing at you!"

I knew what it was. Part of me was still in shock from being caught, but another part stepped back again.

Beefy swore. "You make one more move and I'll fire!"

The gun was a short-barrelled pistol of some sort. I'd played enough first-person shooters to know that it couldn't be very accurate. Not over any sort of distance. From the top of the mound to me was fifty feet. At least that. Not less than forty anyway. Thirty-five, minimum.

I took another step backwards.

"You little bastard!" He took a step towards me, starting on the downward slope, treading carefully on the uneven footing but still keeping his gun pointed at me and with his phone still in the other hand.

I turned and ran.

There was a shout, a bang, a sudden burst of dust and soil from the ground a few feet to my right, and I discovered that I still had some adrenaline left in me. I ran faster, round the edge of the pit, heading for the fence.

Two more shots. I didn't see them hit – more importantly, didn't feel them hit – then there was a scream from behind. I glanced back. Beefy was tumbling down the slope, arms and legs flailing, heading towards the pit.

The fence was twenty feet away. Ten feet away. Just in front of me now. But it was intact here, and six foot high. I followed it, desperation driving me now as the brief surge of energy faded.

There was another shout: another of Canoso's men coming out of the wasteland, gun in hand. He fired. Three or four shots, but he was still a hundred yards away. Bullets were ricocheting off brick and concrete, but none came near me. And there was a gap! An entire section torn from the posts and trampled down. I tripped on the loose wire mesh as I crossed it, somehow kept my feet, staggering across the road.

Where was June? I looked up and down the street. On one side the ruins of Delford Mills. On the other, rows of shuttered houses. No cars.

Behind me, the shooting had stopped, but I could hear the man's footsteps crunching through the rubble as he ran towards me. Up the street, there was movement: a figure in a white shirt clambering over the fence from the wasteland. Canoso.

I crossed the street, desperately scanning the houses for an open door, an unboarded window – anywhere I could run to for cover. I just needed to stay ahead of them for a few minutes. June would come, I was sure of it. This place was supposed to be full of squatters, wasn't it? They had to get in somehow.

There was an alleyway just ahead, an arched entrance leading into darkness between and beneath two of the houses. I made for it at the best speed I could. Behind me, there was a shout. But no more shooting. Perhaps he'd emptied his magazine.

My breath was coming in gasps, each one agonizing, but I couldn't stop panting, not while I was still trying to run. I pushed myself to keep going, and the shadows of the alleyway closed round me. Hiding me.

But not protecting me. They'd seen where I'd gone; they'd be right behind me.

The alleyway was half blocked with rubbish: rotting timbers, plastic bags filled with decay, a bicycle frame. I pulled the frame round, jamming it crosswise between the walls. It might slow them.

There was daylight at the end of the alleyway. I came out into another wilderness, where the tiny gardens and little vegetable plots that had once been the pride and joy of the householders had been left to turn into a miniature jungle. Brambles poured over the low walls on either side, thorns grabbing and tearing at me as I forced my way past.

Ahead of me loomed the backs of more shuttered houses. At one time there had been a maze of little alleys here, giving access to the back gardens and kitchen doors. Now they had all but disappeared under the wild vegetation. The faintest hint of a path still showed where they might have been, and perhaps where squatters had found access. I followed it, holding my hands up to avoid the huge stinging nettles that crowded me on either side.

There was movement behind me. Someone stumbling in the dark alley, swearing loudly as they came across the bike frame.

"Do you see him?" Canoso's voice, shouting from the street.

"No, but he came down here. No place else he could have gone."

"Then you keep after him! And where is Gazza?"

"I haven't seen him."

"He does not answer his phone. No matter. We look for him later. First is to get Seaton out of there."

"OK. I just need to reload."

"Shoot for a leg. I want to talk with him. And then I will kill him myself."

I had kept moving throughout the conversation. The last line was encouragement not to stop. The path was becoming clearer, as if more used at this end. Another path joined it, running towards the back of a house. Perhaps one that had hosted squatters? I couldn't see if it went to an open door or window. But even if it did, I could find myself trapped inside – I'd already seen that there were no openings onto the street. And I had to get back to the street, to meet June.

I kept on, hoping that they would explore the other path. There were noises behind me again: someone forcing their way through the jungle, cursing at the nettles and brambles. They would be able to see me if it weren't for the rampant plant life. They would probably hear me if they weren't making so much noise themselves.

The path split again. Left and right. Left, an apple tree was forcing its way through a wall, half choked with creepers, and the path beyond was impenetrable without a machete. Right led back towards Gladstone Street. At least I thought it did. I was losing my sense of direction, and I didn't have time to try to work it out. My pursuer was right behind me. But which way would he go? Left or right? If he went a different way, I might have a chance to double back, get out onto the street the way I'd come.

That gave me another idea, another option. I went forward. Grabbing a tree branch, I pulled myself up and over the wall, and dropped down the other side into a tiny gap between wall and trunk and brambles. I tried not to scream or even moan as the effort sent new pain stabbing through my chest, because Canoso's man had caught up now. I could hear his heavy breathing just the other side of the wall. He might even have seen me climbing over, in which case I was finished. I struggled to breathe as lightly as possible, not to move or even twitch, as he stood a few feet away, cursing quietly to himself. Then his phone rang.

"Did you get him yet?" Canoso's voice, faint but clear.

"No, boss. There's another fork, and no footprints this time. I don't know which way he went."

I'd left footprints? That was why he was so close behind me. I hadn't even thought of checking the ground.

"Check both ways, then! I will stay here, by the exit, in case he tries to come back this way. Hurry it up!"

So much for my cunning plan.

"Yes, will do." He moved off again, hurrying as instructed. He took the left path.

Which left me only one way to go. I hauled myself back over the wall and this time I couldn't avoid letting out a moan. At least it confirmed that my ribs weren't broken, I told myself. If they had been, I'd have a punctured lung by now and I'd already be dead. Which was the closest I could get to a comforting thought as I made my way down the right-hand path.

A wall emerged from the vegetation in front of me. A shuttered window. A door. The metal cover had been forced off at one time, but re-secured, with bars welded on and padlocked to hasps set deep into the brickwork on either side. Big, heavy-duty padlocks, still shiny and new. It seemed that the authorities had finally got round to dealing with the squatter problem. Lousy timing, from my point of view. But they had at least cleared the path. It ran alongside the house, bramble free, and disappeared into another alleyway. One that would lead to the road.

This one was even darker than the other. There was no light at all coming from the other end, so there was probably a gate or a door. Would it be locked? Bolted? On the inside or the outside? Fortunately, it had been cleared of rubbish. I groped my way along it, gritty brickwork under my fingers, until my forehead met something solid. I reached out and felt smooth steel. When the council workers had come to re-secure the doors at the back, they'd also closed off the way out. Just the one they'd used, obviously, or I would never have got into this maze. Presumably that other alleyway wasn't on the job sheet, or hadn't been budgeted for. So I could get in, but not out.

I leaned against the metal, pushed at it, heard a faint rattle. Like a chain. Probably with another one of those big padlocks. Not something that would give with a bit of a shove. I rested my head on the cool surface, thinking of June coming past on the street outside, driving up and down and wondering where I was. Cut off from me by a single sheet of galvanized steel.

There was a noise behind me, and I turned to see the small amount of light coming down the alleyway obscured by a shadowy figure. He still didn't know I was here. I could creep forward, hidden in the shadows, take him by surprise. Get his gun, perhaps. Or his phone. I could hold Canoso off then, call June, and tell her where I was. I could still win.

But though I thought about it, I was still slumped against the door. I couldn't get my body to move any more. I was finished, done.

There was a sudden bright light. Just a mobile phone screen, but it dazzled me.

"I've got him!" The man sounded both excited and relieved. He'd stopped about halfway down the alley. "Can you hear me?... Yes, I'm in another one of these covered passages; that's why the signal's bad. He's here. The street end's blocked off. Do you want me to drag him out, or are you coming in?... Sorry, boss, what was that?... OK. Do you know which one it is?... OK."

He hung up, and stood still. I wondered what he was doing, but couldn't be bothered to ask.

There was silence for a moment. Then a massive explosion right next to my head. And another. I fell forward thinking I was already dead, but the door squeaked open, letting in brilliant light. I blinked furiously and saw Canoso standing there, gun in hand.

Even a heavy-duty lock was no match for a bullet. The council obviously hadn't thought about squatters with firearms.

"Get him out of there." Canoso's voice.

146

Hands gripped me, dragged me, left me lying on my back, blinking up at the faces: Canoso and his two little helpers. Gazza – the beefy one – had apparently found his way out of the pit he had fallen into. A pity. I'd hoped he'd been buried in the rubble. But at least he wasn't unscathed; his shirt was torn and his face was covered in blood and truculence.

"You are so much a troublemaker, Mr Seaton," Canoso said. His voice was tight and angry, and his accent was stronger. "But what – you think it makes any difference? You think you escape from me like this? You think I just let you run away – and with my sister's bag? With evidence against me?"

Laney's bag was still hanging from my shoulder. He nodded at Gazza, who reached down and pulled it off, not trying to be gentle about it. Canoso searched through it with one hand, while Gazza held it open.

"And you take some of my merchandise as well?" He held up the packaged Lappies. "You think, perhaps, you will show these to the police?"

He put the packages back in the bag and turned to me again. "So. The code for the door. How did you know this?" He pointed his gun directly at my head as he spoke. The sun must have come out, because I could see shiny highlights on the metal. I concentrated on them. It suddenly seemed important to notice every detail. To experience every moment.

"Do not ignore me, Mr Seaton. This is rude." He crouched, reached out with his gun, and rapped me on the head with the barrel.

I looked at him. His face was still bloody, though it had dried now.

"That's better. Now then, I asked you a question. How did you know the code to open the door?"

"We should get going," one of his men said, looking round. "Someone might have heard those shots. Coppers could be on their way. Let's finish him and clear off."

"Who is in this place to hear anything? A few tramps – perhaps some squatters. They will not involve themselves. We have plenty of time to ask questions." He dug the barrel under my chin. "Well, Mr Seaton?"

I couldn't fight any more. I was too tired now; I just wanted it to finish. "Laney knew," I whispered.

"Yes, I showed her myself when I convinced her to join me. But how did *you* know? Did she tell you?"

"No. Never met her. It was in her poem. The one she sent to the library."

"I saw that. She wrote nothing of the door, and there were no numbers."

"It was all about the door, and the pub, and what was behind the door. You just had to know how to read it."

He shook his head, muttering something in Spanish. "This is annoying. I should have paid more attention to the poem. Still, I now understand why she took La Paz before she killed herself. She knew the police would test her body for drugs, and hoped it would point them to me."

"It did. They're on to you, Canoso. They know you're involved, and when they read the poem they'll know where to look."

"But who will read it?" He searched my pockets till he found the crumpled piece of paper. "Of course, I understand what you are thinking now. You're thinking of the copy the librarian made. Such a helpful lady! When I explained that I was a member of the family, she was so pleased to show it to me. And when I go back and ask for all the copies, I expect she will give them to me."

"She'll go to the police if something happens to me," I said desperately, and Canoso laughed.

"But nothing will happen to you, Mr Seaton! You will go away, that is all. And your boss will wonder why you do not come to work, your landlord will come looking for the rent, and the police will search and make inquiries – but no one will find you." He made a broad gesture, taking in the abandoned houses and the ruins of the Mills. "There are so many places where you could be, after all."

He leaned forward and dropped his voice. "And shall I tell you something more? Explain to you what you do not know? You find out much, but understand very little. The police will not investigate my sister any more. They will not have any more interest in La Paz."

I was struggling to stay with the conversation. There was too much pain, too much exhaustion, and I just wanted to be left alone. But some last little bit of survival instinct was telling me to keep talking, keep him talking, because once he stopped I was dead. And if he would just talk a little bit longer, June would come. She would be here.

And besides, he had just said something important. I frowned, trying to concentrate. "Why not?" I forced the words out.

"You see? You do not know as much as you thought, Mr Seaton." He was smiling now, his good humour fully restored. "Do you not wonder why the police take such interest in you when Laney dies, but take no notice of me? Did you know that they watch your flat, but not my pub?"

I stared at him. "How do you know…" Just in time I remembered that I wasn't supposed to be aware of the surveillance. "Why would they be watching my flat?"

"Because I told them to!"

And now that it had been spelled out for me, it was all obvious. "You have someone in the police!"

He nodded, chuckling as if I had finally understood a joke. "My father, he taught me this. Always to have a man in the police. Never to begin an operation without it. And so when I came here, I knew that I would be under suspicion once La Paz appeared on the streets. So I first sought for a suitable person who would help things run smoothly. You have met him, I believe. DS Fayden?"

I thought of Mickey Fayden and his expensive suits, his top-of-the-range car, and his high opinion of himself. "He came to interview me. Asked me about drugs."

"Yes, that is the one. I arranged with him to have the Prince William raided. Of course, nothing was found, so I was in the clear and could proceed with my operation."

"But Laney messed that up."

He shook his head. "She was a disappointment to me – as she was to our father. Family did not mean anything to her. She even threatened to tell the police about me, can you believe?" He smiled. "Ah, but there is a joke here – I'm sure this will amuse you, Mr Seaton – I had the police watching her to be sure that she would not tell the police!"

He chuckled, but I couldn't even manage a grin. "I don't get it."

"What? You do not see? And you British are so proud of your sense of humour. It is simple. I do not know if I can trust my sister. So I arrange for my good friend Mickey to have her watched. So if she tries to go to the police, he is the first to know. He is the one she tells. And the story goes no further. And then, of course, I let her know that she is watched. I tell her it is for her own good, so that when she works for me she has already been cleared of suspicion. But of course, she understood, and she did not try to tell the police."

"I wondered why she didn't. I put it down to a family history of distrusting authority – quite reasonable, considering. But you'd closed that off for her. She didn't give up, though, did she? She found another way. Dosed herself with your drug and wrote that poem as a clue. One she knew you wouldn't understand. And then…"

"Yes, then she goes to the road, chooses your vehicle, and walks into your path. This I know. But still I do not understand why would she do such a thing? Why does she fight so hard against me that she must even kill herself? She had no need to die. I promised to pay her well, to give her a good life, her and her grandmother. She could write her poems, publish her books – I would not stop her. It is…"

DAY 8: THE BEGINNING

Canoso ran out of words, and raised his arms in helpless bafflement. I thought of trying to explain everything I'd heard from Roshawn, but I was too tired, and he still wouldn't get it anyway. Instead, I had a question of my own.

"What I don't understand is why you had Fayden come after me. All those questions and the surveillance... he knew I wasn't involved! What was the point?"

Canoso shrugged. "It was important that he was seen to be doing something. He must be busy, so that his superiors let him continue to be in charge. So I tell him to watch you for a while. And then you will disappear, and in your flat they find La Paz. So – it seems that Mickey was right all along, and he gets his promotion. The matter of my sister's death is finished, and if La Paz is still circulating, well, that must be down to you. They will look for you a long time, I think!"

He smiled and smiled, watching my face as I grappled with his meaning and finally came to understand. "You were going to kill me anyway. You had already planned it."

He nodded with enthusiasm. "Ah, now you have it. A good plan, is it not? Especially as I had to think very quickly when my sister was so foolish as to die – and with La Paz in her blood as well, that made matters more difficult. But you were most convenient. A man without family, without attachments. A man who could easily disappear. And also the man who killed my sister, so it is a personal matter as well. Of course, I did not expect you to come to me and make all this difficulty. But, then again, you have saved me the trouble of coming to find you. It is wonderful how well things work out sometimes, is it not?"

I didn't really see it that way, but there was something else that I wanted to get clear in my head. "Fayden leaked the post-mortem results to you? That's how you knew that Laney had taken La Paz?"

"Of course." He looked at me, suddenly suspicious. "But how do you know about the post-mortem?"

June had told me. But if he found that out, then he would want

151

to know what else she knew. And I suddenly realized that if I was dead, she'd be the only person with any chance of unravelling this mess and stopping him. Canoso couldn't know about her.

"The post-mortem?" I asked stupidly.

"Yes. You will tell me what you know of this, or I will make things very bad for you."

Worse than they already were? I saw the look in his eyes, and believed that, yes, that might be possible. "I... heard about it."

"Who from?"

"I... you said it. In the cellar. You said then that she had taken La Paz. You already knew. So I thought it must have been from the post-mortem. I knew that there had been one, but I didn't know what the results were. No one did; they hadn't been released. But you knew, so you must have heard, and it must have been from Fayden."

He looked at me for a moment. Then shrugged. "Well, that was clever of you. But no matter. What you know is no longer important. And now that I have explained why you must die, it is time to finish this."

He stood up and aimed at my head.

I didn't believe it. Even though I could see it happening, I couldn't really believe I was about to die. It just wasn't possible for things simply to come to an end.

"No... no, wait a minute," I protested, desperate to stop him, to hold him back, even for just a moment, just another second of life.

And I could hear a car. Revving hard, getting louder.

He shook his head. "Waiting is over. Goodbye, Mr Seaton."

There was a tortured shriek, rubber on tarmac, a sudden jump in the engine noise as the car came round a corner. I couldn't see it, but Canoso and his men could. They were looking up the street, and Gazza said, "It's the cops! Leg it!"

Then he was off and running, the other one following. But Canoso had turned and was aiming at the car, firing two quick shots before I kicked him in the back of the leg. The third bullet went high in the air as he fell to his left, turning as he did so, and I saw his face, the fury directed at me, just before the car reached us.

Then he was gone.

The yellow and blue stripe went past a foot from my nose, tyres smoking and flinging grit in my face. It finally came to a stop several yards further down the street, leaving blood and torn flesh and smoking rubber in its wake. And déjà vu in my head.

There was a conversation going on in the background, someone on the radio. I thought I recognized a voice, but I was too tired, too drained to look. I lay staring up at the clouds, until June bent over me.

"Rob! Rob! Did he shoot you? Did I hit you? Speak to me, Rob!" Her hands were on my face, searching my body, checking me for bullet holes in a professional manner while her eyes dripped unprofessional tears on my chest.

"Easy there," I whispered. "It's not a date."

DAY 9: MOVING ON

I was amazed by the number of visitors I got in hospital. Colin came, and several of my driving mates – who I would have expected. But to my surprise Liz and some other office staff turned up too. Sandra came from the library, and Roshawn as well. Both of them wanted to pray for me, which was a little embarrassing but also rather moving.

Less welcome was the copper who came to take my statement. I'd been expecting it, of course, and managed to give a good account of events without mentioning my non-date with June or any of the information I'd got from her. On the other hand, I didn't get much information back, either. I asked several times about Mickey Fayden, but the most I could get was that he was "being sought for".

So he'd done a runner – probably as soon as he heard that Canoso was dead. That was more information than had appeared in the very sparse press reports, which merely indicated that the police had found a "drugs factory" following an "incident". No mention of La Paz, no links to Laney, and my name was kept out of it this time. The clear instruction from the copper was that I should keep it that way, and I wasn't inclined to argue.

The person I most wanted to see didn't appear. June sent me a text, telling me she was OK and she'd be along when she could. Nothing more. I sent her texts, I left messages on her voicemail, but there was no reply. Well, it happens. It does to me, anyhow, and I had no good reason to believe this was any different. After all, we hardly knew each other.

It turned out that I'd suffered a lot less damage than I should have, considering all the high-velocity lead flying around. I had two cracked ribs, some cuts from flying glass, and a magnificent set of bruises all over my face and body. The CSI who came to photograph them was thrilled by the wonderful colours and contrasts; it was the highlight of his day. I still hurt everywhere, but the doctor assured me that everything was healing nicely, and sent me home with appropriate strapping and strong painkillers.

I was just in the slow and careful process of getting dressed when June showed up. They'd put me in my own room off the main ward, probably because of the statement being taken, so there was no curtain round the bed. Fortunately, I'd got my trousers on when she opened the door and peered through.

"Escaping already?" she asked.

"Apparently I'm taking up bed space."

"Looks like I got here just in time then."

"You're good at that."

She smiled. "So can I come in?"

"Might as well, since you've already violated my privacy."

"Oh. Sorry about that. The nurse said you should be finished by now."

"I'm taking things slow. Have a seat." I indicated the visitor's chair, while I remained sitting on the bed, buttoning my shirt. She wasn't in uniform. "So this isn't an official visit, then?" I asked as she sat down.

"Semi-official. I'm allowed to come and say thanks for saving my life when you kicked Canoso off balance."

"I think we're even on that score. Your timing was perfect. Though a few minutes earlier would have saved me a bit of stress!"

"Sorry about that. It was several miles of heavy traffic from the station, and I didn't have authorization for 'blues and twos'. If I'd known there were guns involved…"

"They hadn't started shooting when I called you. I didn't even know they had guns, though I suppose I should have guessed. I wouldn't have got you shot at if I'd known…"

"He missed. So forget it."

"But how close did he come?"

"The first bullet went through the near-side windscreen and punched a hole in the passenger seat headrest."

"Good thing you didn't have a passenger!"

"Nobody at the station will travel with me now. I think they're joking…" She grinned and shook her head. "The second one hit about a foot further left, near the centre of the windscreen, and it went straight through the car and out of the back." She reached up to touch a small red line on her cheek, just below her left eye. "It flung some glass around as well. But that was as close as he got."

"Bad shooting, or just good luck, do you think?"

"Well, there is a theory going round the station that Canoso, being Spanish, instinctively aimed at the wrong side of the car. Thank God for right-hand drive, eh? Actually, I think he was just trying to scare me off, at least with the first shot. He would have seen me clearly enough through the windscreen."

A thought came to me: a memory of sunshine glinting on a gun barrel, and I felt a cold chill. "He couldn't see you," I whispered.

"What?"

"He couldn't see you," I repeated. "The sun had just come out. It was shining on his gun. And it would have been on your windscreen, June. He wouldn't have been able to see through the glare. He was firing blind and trying to kill you."

"Oh." She looked thoughtful. "Thanks for clarifying that. But perhaps best not to mention it. The whole thing's complicated enough as it is. You wouldn't believe the paperwork generated by a little bump in a police car!"

"Are you in any trouble over that? I mean – it was a fatal RTC, wasn't it?"

"Well, yes. But I didn't see him fall in front of the car – my vision was obscured by the bullet holes in the windscreen, of course."

"Sounds reasonable to me." I reached out my hand. "Thanks, June."

"Thank *you*, Rob. And you're welcome."

We shook hands, very formally, but neither of us let go.

"June – I was wondering…" I paused. I'd practised this numerous times over the past few days but still couldn't find the words. "When I'm feeling up to it, could we perhaps get together sometime?"

"You mean, for a date?"

I felt a surge of hope, so strong that it was painful. Especially round my ribs. "Or even a non-date?"

The hope crashed and died as she shook her head and let go of my hand. "Rob, we've talked about this, remember? Unprofessional conduct. I can't date you, end of."

"Oh. I see."

"Of course, if we happened to see each other by coincidence, that would be different."

I raised an eyebrow. "What sort of coincidence?"

"Well, for example, I'm going to see my nephew in a school play in a couple of weeks. If you were there as well, and we happened to bump into each other – well, these things happen." She met my gaze and matched my raised eyebrow. "Of course, it might not be your sort of thing."

"Perhaps not. But then again, I've been taking an interest in poetry lately. Perhaps I should look at drama as well. What's the play?"

"It's a musical, actually. It's called 'Where's Sally?'. I hear it's quite good."

"Sounds like just my sort of thing."

"Alderman Baird School, Thursday evening performance. Don't be late."

I nodded, grinning. "I'll be there. And what about just now? Are you busy?"

She gave me a stern look. "Don't push it."

"No, I wouldn't do that. It's just that I've been discharged… and I could use a lift home, if that's allowed?"

"Hmm. I suppose I can get away with it. Under the circumstances. Is this your bag? You probably shouldn't be carrying anything heavy until those ribs are healed."

"Thank you, officer. Much appreciated."

We left the room together.

Last night I thought I saw Laney again, stepping out in front of me, looking so calm and peaceful. But this time, she spoke.

"I'm sorry," she said.

"It's all right, Laney," I told her. "It's all right."

COMING IN OCTOBER
2017

LOCAL
ARTIST

Whet your appetite with Chapter 1…

CHAPTER 1

A phone call at four in the morning is rarely a good thing. Especially when it's from the police.

I fumbled through the clutter on my bedside table, found my mobile, and jabbed my finger at the screen, more or less at random, until the noise stopped.

"What?" I muttered.

"Hello? Is that Sandra? Sandra Deeson?"

"Um."

"Sandra, this is June Henshaw. Sergeant Henshaw. From Central Police Station?"

"Um. Yes. June." I knew her slightly.

"Sorry to bother you at this time, but we've got your name and number as keyholder for the library on Bromwell Street?"

My brain fog started to clear. "Yes. Yes, that's right. Has something happened?"

"We're not sure, but an officer has discovered an insecurity at the library. We need to gain access to find out what's happened. Would you be able to come down and meet us there?"

"Yes. Of course. I'll be…" I paused, trying to focus my thoughts. It could take an hour to get to work in rush hour traffic, but at this time the roads would be quiet. "Half an hour."

"That's great. Thank you, Sandra. I'll meet you there."

Graham had rolled over in bed and was peering in my direction. "Who was that?" he muttered.

"June Henshaw."

"Rob's girlfriend?"

"Yes, but she had her police hat on. Helmet on. Whatever. Something's up at the library. I need to go and open up for them."

"Want me to come with you?" He was already half out of bed.

"No, love; no need for that. I just need to drive down there and open the doors. And you're supposed to be avoiding stress, remember?"

"Nothing stressful about a phone call from the police at this time of the morning."

"My call, my stress. Really, love, you don't need to bother yourself. Go back to sleep. I'll be back for breakfast."

He gave me a long, if still bleary, look. "OK. If you're sure. Call me if you need an emergency flask of coffee rushing to the scene, or anything like that."

I nodded. "It'll be fine."

I fumbled for some clothes, made my way downstairs. The dog raised his head and wagged a hopeful tail.

"You go back to sleep as well, Brodie."

Nevertheless, he got out of his basket and followed me to the shoe cupboard, to make sure I wasn't sneaking out in walking boots. I slipped on my trainers, and he wandered grumpily back.

Clear skies, cold night. I wished I'd had time to make a coffee, but I'd just have to manage without. I pulled a woolly hat over my head, making a mental note not to take it off under any circumstances, as my hair was a mess, then found my keys and went out.

Even without the coffee, the sharpness of the night air began to wake me up, and the empty roads gave me opportunity to think. And the first coherent thought that came to me was: "Why didn't the alarm go off?" If there had been an intruder in the library, I should have been woken up by the company that monitored the alarm, not the police.

I'd locked up myself last night. Hadn't I? I was sure I was the last one to leave. I'd been helping the art club set up for their exhibition. It was supposed to open this morning… they'd been fussing over their displays, arguing over who got the best positions. Closing time was six, but it had been nearly eight before I managed to usher the last of them out.

The ring road was a fifty-mile-an-hour limit, but I felt no guilt at doing sixty. Maybe sixty-five. But I was responding to a police emergency, wasn't I? And in any case, there was no one else on it. One set of headlights passed on the other side of the dual carriageway, some huge artic lumbering through the night, but I had the rest of the road to myself.

I was sure I'd set the alarm. It made a horrendous high-pitched warbling sound when you did, to let you know you had ten seconds to get out of the building. Since the panel was right next to the exit, that wasn't a problem, but it still made me panic slightly. And it was impossible to forget to do it.

Or was it? If I hadn't set the alarm and there had been a break in…

Worrying about that, I nearly failed to stop at the red lights as I came off the ring road. Not a residential area, fortunately, or the screech of rubber on road might have woken someone. Why were the lights red at that time? There was nothing else moving.

Having enjoyed their little joke with me, the lights reluctantly allowed me to go on my way. Down through the industrial estate and out onto Lock Road.

No, I must have set the alarm. So that meant nobody had actually got in, then. Perhaps just some drunk causing damage to the door or a window. Years ago, when we were more lax about security, someone had left a fire escape door open. We'd come in next morning and found an inebriated gentleman sleeping it off in the reference section. He was very apologetic when he woke up and realized where he was. Didn't remember how he'd got there.

That must be it, I thought. No actual burglary. Panic over.

All the same, it still made my stomach churn when I finally

turned onto Bromwell Street and saw two police cars pulled up in front of the library.

As I parked behind them, a police officer got out and walked towards me. I wouldn't have recognized June if I hadn't been expecting her: in fleece and stab vest she looked stocky, and the blonde hair that normally framed her face was pulled back into a ponytail.

"No blue lights?" I asked.

"On the off chance that someone was still inside, we didn't want to alert them. Of course, they're probably long gone, if anyone was there at all. Still, we need to be sure, so thanks for coming out, Sandra."

"Well, I didn't want you kicking the door in!" I meant it as a joke, but tiredness made it come out sharper than I intended. I forced a smile. "Not that you would, of course."

"We try to avoid it wherever possible." June showed no sign of offence, but of course she was used to dealing with much worse than grumpy middle-aged librarians. "In this case, we're not even sure that there has been any illegal entry, so we weren't about to cause any unnecessary damage."

The word "damage" drew my eyes to the library itself, wondering just what harm might have been done.

About a hundred and fifty years ago, a local businessman had been inspired to build a great edifice of learning and enlightenment. And self-importance (it was to be named the Arthur Diogenes Bromwell Institute of Culture). However, his lofty vision came into conflict with his natural inclination to save a bob or two wherever he could. The result was a single-storey red-brick building, high windows facing the street, blank walls along the back, and a massively oversized front entrance, all columns, brass plaques, and Latin inscriptions. The double doors were ten feet high, oak and stained glass. In short it was a fine example of Victorian Monstrosity. Various mismatched additions accumulated over the years as needs dictated and funds enabled, improving functionality but doing nothing for appearance.

It was hard to see details in the dim street lighting, but everything looked as solid, secure, and ugly as normal. I raised an eyebrow in June's direction.

"It's round the back," she explained, and led the way. "We got a call from a member of the public about an hour ago, telling us something was happening here. PC Newbold (she indicated the young copper who had joined her) came to have a look round, and he found an open window."

We came to the narrow alley between the library on one side and a block of flats on the other. June shone a torch down it. "Mike, you stay and watch the front, just in case someone tries to do a runner. Are you OK with this, Sandra?"

"Of course. I doubt if anyone's actually got in, or the alarm would have been activated."

"You're probably right, and if anyone *was* here I expect they made off when Mike showed up. But there might be somebody lurking around at the back, so stay behind me and if anything kicks off, don't get involved, OK?"

We walked down the alley, the only illumination coming from June's torch. I told myself to stop feeling so nervous. I'd come this way every working day for twenty years, after all. Just not at night with the police.

The red Victorian brickwork gave way to the grey blocks of the Children's Section, a 1950s addition. "Was it someone from the flats who reported it?" I asked.

"We don't know. Anonymous call from the TK down the road. Telephone kiosk, that is. Long gone by the time we got here. But I'm not sure how much of the library you can see from the flats; there are no windows directly overlooking it."

We came to the end of the Children's Section, followed the path round the back, and came out on a scrappy bit of lawn. Ahead of us was the toilet block, built in the late eighties to replace the original facilities.

"Just there." June shone her torch, indicating a transom

window sticking out rebelliously when it should have been flush with the wall.

"Ladies' loo. Is that big enough for someone to get in?"

June shrugged. "You don't get many fat burglars. You'd be surprised at the holes they can wiggle through. Could it have been left open by accident?"

I thought back. "I locked up, but it was quite late, and I didn't check everywhere. One of my staff had done that earlier, but I suppose it's possible that someone came in and opened a window afterwards. The art club were here all evening – though I don't know why they'd open a window."

"The windows aren't alarmed?"

"Not here. There are sensors in all the rooms, though, and the corridor."

She looked more closely at the window. "No sign of any forced entry. Screwdrivers or crowbars leave marks, especially in UPVC like this. OK, let's go inside. Which door do we use?"

"Round here." I led the way to the bottom end of the toilet block. "The main entrance is bolted from the inside; the back door is easier."

I fumbled with my keys. The door had both a Yale and a solid mortise lock. I opened them both, and paused with my fingers on the handle.

"The alarm panel's on the wall just next to the door. The delay is quite short, so I'll go straight in and turn it off. Then you can go ahead and look round – OK?"

June nodded. I pushed the handle down and the door in. Strip lights automatically began flickering into life as I stepped through, turned sharp right, and put my hand out to the keypad.

It wasn't there.

For a moment I stood and waved my hands in empty space, glancing round in bemusement. Was I in the wrong place? Was this even the right door? Then I registered the holes in the wall where the screws had been, plaster dust leaking out and a bent Rawlplug showing. I glanced down, and saw the shattered plastic box with broken wires trailing from it.

"June…" I began, but she was already through the door behind me. "Wait outside please, Sandra." She keyed her radio. "November Delta one-five to HQ. Confirmed break at Bromwell Library."

"Ten-four. Do you need back-up?"

"No sign of anyone still here at present, but if November Charlie three-six has finished booking her prisoner in, you can send her over."

"Three-six. Got that, sarge. On my way."

"Thanks. November Charlie four-two, receiving?"

"Four-two. Do you want me to join you, sarge?" Mike's voice.

"Not yet. Cover the front till Sara arrives, then come round the back. I'm going to stay here till then."

"Roger that."

June stepped back out through the door. "Do you want to go and wait at the car?"

I thought of finding my way back through the alley, which would be pitch black without June's torch. Of course, I could ask her to escort me, but then if there was anyone still in the building, that would have given them an opportunity to escape.

I shook my head. "No, I'm fine. I expect you'll want me to see if anything's missing when you go in?"

"Once we've checked it's clear. This shouldn't take long. Sara – PC Middleton – is only about ten minutes away."

It was a very long ten minutes. We waited in silence, June carefully scanning all the other visible windows and listening intently. But the silence was unbroken except by the buzz from one of the fluorescent tubes and the occasional message coming over June's radio. I had to restrain myself from jumping every time I heard it crackle.

It was a good thing Graham hadn't come, I decided. This was definitely tense, and I could imagine how he'd fret if he was sitting in the car waiting for me. Not doctor's orders at all.

My phone pinged, another pluck on my overstretched nerves. I fumbled for it, my chain of thought leading me to expect Graham, checking up on me.

"Message?" asked June. "From the alarm company?"

I located the phone, deep in the most inaccessible pocket, unzipped several layers, and finally managed to pull it out.

"No. Just my 'Daily Eloquence'."

"Daily *what*?"

"It's a website I subscribe to. They text me an 'Eloquent Word for the Day' every morning. Usually something obscure. The game is that I've then got to use it in conversation sometime that day, and post it online. There's a sort of points system for the best use of the word, and you get a prize if you come out top over the month – a dictionary, usually!"

"That sounds like…" June obviously didn't want to say what she thought, but couldn't quite bring herself to say something polite and meaningless.

"Sounds weird, I know! Don't worry. Graham tells me that every day. I tell him, 'No, it sounds eldritch!'" I gave her a hopeful look, but June just raised an eyebrow. Someday, that's going to get a laugh. "Never mind. I'm a word-nerd, that's all."

"OK. So what's today's word?"

I glanced at the screen again. "Lollygagging."

"Lolly-gagging? Choking on a lollipop?"

"No. It's an American word, I think. It means 'to spend time aimlessly, to dawdle or be idle, to procrastinate or avoid work'."

"As in lying around, doing nothing? I can think of a few people I could apply that to. But not this morning, I hope… that sounds like Sara arriving."

"November Charlie three-six, State 6 at the library."

A few moments later, PC Newbold appeared. With firm instructions for me to stay there until told otherwise, the two officers pulled on disposable gloves and went inside.

The silly conversation over words had relieved some of the

tension, but standing round on my own brought it back. I always had suffered from an excess of imagination, and my mind, running in neutral, quickly began to offer increasingly bizarre scenarios for what they might find. When I reached "terrorist incident" I decided that enough was enough. I had to do something before I progressed to "alien wormholes". And I'd been wondering about that open window. I knew it was the ladies' loo, but which part did it actually open from?

I crept forward, ready to turn and run if anyone not the fuzz came out of the main library. The ladies and gents had both been checked by the coppers on their way in – I'd seen them do that – so at least I knew that no one was hiding in there. Therefore it was safe to proceed that far, at least – or so I told myself.

There were three doors along the corridor, all on the right: cleaner's store nearest the exit, then the ladies, then the gents. The store was locked, as it should be. I progressed a few more steps, and eased open the door to the ladies.

The lights flickered on automatically as I stepped in, showing the sinks directly in front of me, a row of cubicles running off to the left. The windows over the sinks were firmly closed, which didn't surprise me. With taps, basins, and soap dispensers in the way, they were awkward to get at and probably hadn't been opened since they were installed.

I went to the first cubicle and – remembering just in time that this was a crime scene – pushed it open with my elbow. I had read enough detective novels in my time to know not to leave my fingerprints on the door handles.

Sure enough, the window above the toilet was wide open.

These windows would be easy to reach if you stood on the toilet seat. Anyone climbing in would probably have trod there as well. I peered at the plastic lid, trying to make out any footprints, but the positioning of the strip lights put it in shadow. I stepped forward for a closer look, and the door swung shut behind me with a bang that made my heart lurch.

"Sandra?" I heard June call. "Are you all right?"

"Yes, I'm OK, no problems!" I reached for the handle, stopped myself, and pulled at the top of the door, hoping that the intruder hadn't followed the same thought process.

The door was stuck. I remembered then that we'd had trouble with this particular door before. Last winter an old lady had been in here for twenty minutes before someone heard her banging. They'd supposedly fixed the problem – but not completely, it seemed. I heaved on it, and it came free suddenly. I nearly fell back onto the toilet seat but managed to hold myself upright on the door. After regaining my balance I scampered out, nearly running into June.

"I told you to stay by the door!" she said sharply.

"Yes, sorry. I was just, er, checking for any damage. I didn't touch any handles, though."

She shook her head. "My CSI colleagues tell me that they rarely get anything useful from handles anyway. Too small, too well used. What *did* you touch?"

So much for detective novels. "Just the top of the door."

I pointed, and she ran a professional eye over the relevant area. "I'll mention that to CSI. You'd better come through and have a look in the main library. We haven't found anyone, but there's a bit of a mess, and some locked doors we'd like you to check."

I followed on, abashed.

The lights in the main room weren't on sensors, as they were in the newer areas. The coppers had been using their torches, but with a nod from June I switched everything on, and saw what June had called "a bit of a mess".

The main reception desk had been trashed. Every drawer was out, contents emptied over the floor, the files pulled out of the cupboards behind and tossed around, computer screens smashed and hanging from their leads.

June gave me a moment to take it in, and gently restrained me from stepping too close. "There might be footwear marks on the paper," she explained. "Was there anything of value kept here?"

I shook my head. "No, not really. Just paperwork, records, forms – junk, a lot of it. Some of those files are decades old, pre-computerization; we've never got round to archiving everything."

"Do you keep any cash on the premises?"

"A bit. Payment for events and so on… Oh! I just remembered! The art club charge their members to display in the exhibition – just a small amount, but some paid in cash. Might have been a hundred pounds in notes or coins. And the library has a petty cash tin as well. But that's all kept in a safe in my office."

"We'd better check that."

I led the way through the aisles to the Children's Section – the only two-storey part of the building. A door labelled "Staff Only" led up to an office and a staff room. It was securely locked and apparently undamaged. Nevertheless, June inspected it carefully before I unlocked it, and she led the way upstairs.

"All clear," she called back down to Mike. No damage, no one lurking in the shadows, safe untouched.

"Just one more area to check, then."

We went back down the stairs and across to the other side of the library.

At one time there had been a little alcove here, which had been kept free of books to provide space for readings, workshops, and exhibitions. Now there was a rather grand set of sliding doors where the wall had been: pale wood, nicely grained and polished, surmounted by a neat brass plaque announcing it to be "The Laney Grey Memorial Wing". Very fitting – our famous local poet had been a regular user of the alcove before her tragic death. She would have loved the new room, though she'd have poked fun at the idea of a memorial wing.

"Just finished last month. This art exhibition is the first major event we've had here," I said.

"I know. I was at the opening," June reminded me.

"Oh yes, of course you were. Sorry, it was such a hectic day."

June nodded, and moved closer to the door. "Was this here

before, Sandra?" She pointed to a small mark just above the handle.

I looked at it and frowned. On closer inspection, the mark was a rounded indentation in the wood. "I don't think so. I don't remember seeing it before. Of course, it's all still quite new..."

"There's another one. Two more, in fact." June indicated two places, one higher up than the first one, the other further down. "Could be tool marks. But they're only on one side. If someone had pushed a screwdriver in and tried to lever the doors open, you'd expect to see marks on both sides."

I shook my head. "I suppose they might have been there before and I just haven't noticed them. Might have been something done when they were made. A local company donated them free, so we weren't going to be overly critical."

"I'll have a closer look with the doors open." June tugged on the handle with her gloved hand. "Still seems secure, so I doubt if anyone got in. Burglars don't usually lock up behind themselves."

"Actually, they wouldn't have to," I said. "These doors are on an automatic system. They detect movement in and out. After thirty minutes, if nobody goes through, they automatically close and lock themselves. It's a security feature, to stop them being left open by accident. Of course, you can lock them open permanently, but you need to put in a different code."

June raised an eyebrow. "Very sophisticated!"

"Yes – a bit over the top for a library, but I think the manufacturers were getting the maximum publicity out of it. They made a big thing about all the features; we've been in trade magazines all over the world, apparently."

"Who knew the codes?"

"All the library staff, of course. The manufacturers, I suppose. I can't think of anyone else who would have had them."

PC Newbold spoke up. "Have you seen this, sarge?" He was pointing his torch into the corner, where the beam highlighted a small, pale object.

171

"Cigarette end? Good spot, Mike. You don't have anyone smoking in here, do you, Sandra?"

I shook my head firmly. "Of course not!"

"Good! Could be our burglar, then." She crouched down for a closer look, and sniffed. "No sign of burning on the carpet, no smell of smoke. But it hasn't been stubbed out, either. Burnt down to the filter. Curious."

"Might have been walked in on someone's shoe…" Mike suggested.

"Doesn't look crushed." June stood up again. "We'll leave it for CSI to collect and send in for DNA. I'll try and get them to come as soon as possible, Sandra, to minimize the disruption, but they don't start until eight, so I'm afraid you'll probably have to stay closed for the morning at least."

"That'll be a disappointment for the art club, but I'm sure they'll understand. We can rearrange things, I suppose."

"Thanks. That would be helpful. We'd better check the exhibition, just to be thorough. How do we get in?"

I flipped open a discreet panel next to the doors, revealing a keypad. "This looks OK. Shall I go ahead and open it?"

"Let me do it." June stepped over. "I don't think they can get fingerprints off this surface, but no harm in being careful." She poised a gloved finger over the numbers. "What's the code?"

"Five-three-nine-one."

June punched in the numbers as I spoke them. The lock disengaged with a distinct click and the doors slid smoothly open, the lights coming on as they did so.

PC Newbold swore, softly but distinctly.

In order to maximize display space, the new wing had been designed without windows. Instead, the curving roof was all toughened glass, to give the greatest possible amount of natural light – with discreet lighting to give the same effect at night.

The lighting had been another contribution from a local company, and it worked perfectly. Every display stand, every

CHAPTER 1

painting and collage and sculpture, was brilliantly illuminated, with no shadows to hide anyone's work. Even the empty display directly in front of the door was bright and distinct.

As was the man lying sprawled face down on the floor in a pool of red.

DEEP WATER

"An intelligent, thought-provoking read, with engaging and believable characters. It gripped me from the start, and didn't let go."
Sarah Rayne, author of
What Lies Beneath

A CURE FOR OBESITY, WORTH BILLIONS.

A DEATH IN A CLINICAL TRIAL.

When patent lawyer Daniel Marchmont agrees to act for Calliope Biotech, he doesn't know what he's getting into. The first lawyer on the case is dead, and a vital lab book is missing.

Daniel and his wife Rachel are hoping biotechnology will also provide a cure for their daughter Chloe, who suffers from a devastating genetic disorder. Then the unimaginable happens, and they face a moral dilemma that threatens everything.

Meanwhile young researcher Katie Flanagan suspects something is very wrong in the lab. But knowledge is dangerous when someone is playing a perilous game...

ISBN: 978 1 78264 214 5 | e-ISBN: 978 1 78264 215 2